I Knew

IN A

Moment

I Knew
IN A
Moment

CONNOR FALLS CHRISTMAS SERIES
BOOK TWO

Robin Maderich

POTTER STREET BOOKS
ZIONSVILLE PA
2024

ISBN: 979-8-9914596-2-4

© 2024 Robin Maderich
All rights reserved.

Printed in the U.S.A.

Cover design by Robin Maderich

Potter Street Books/Robin Maderich Publishing
www.potterstreetbooks.com

This book is also available in digital format.

"My idea of Christmas, whether old-fashioned
or modern, is very simple: loving others.
Come to think of it, why do we have
to wait for Christmas to do that?"
— **Bob Hope**

AUTHOR'S NOTE

We all suffer grief and loss in our lives. We also experience wonder and joy. At Christmastime, those emotions can, and often do, grow stronger.

In *I Knew in a Moment*, book two of the Connor Falls Christmas series, I have explored all of those emotions and more. Not in a way to overwhelm, but like an underscore to what is beautiful in life. There will possibly be tears as you read, but not sad ones. Ones that make us remember what is precious. Then again, perhaps I am thinking too much, expecting too much from words on paper. But I don't think so.

Merry Christmas, everyone. Happy reading!

Chapter One

Nikki fished through her purse for her wallet, cheeks heating as she realized she had left it in her car. Pushing a gloved hand through her windblown hair, she apologized. "I'm sorry. I...I'll be right back. I've forgotten my wallet in the console."

The woman on the opposite side of the bakery counter smiled. Not a knowing, I-bet-you-have smile but more like she understood, had possibly been there herself once or twice. "I'll bag up your cookies and set them right here."

"I'm parked at the end of the block," Nikki explained.

"Your cookies aren't going anywhere and neither am I."

Nikki left From the Hart bakery, the jangling bells over the door calling attention to her exit. This was probably the point where people became too embarrassed to return and snuck off into oblivion, leaving their purchases behind. Nikki didn't have that luxury. For one thing, she planned on sticking around in this town for a little bit, and she hadn't noted any other bakery on her drive in. For another, she'd been told to ask for Gina Hart, the bakery owner, and Nikki felt fairly certain the attractive, dark-haired woman behind the counter was Gina.

"Ah, fudge," she muttered, hustling along the sidewalk in daylight's last glow to the metered space where she had parked her car. She pressed the key fob to unlock it, yanked open the door and leaned across the passenger seat. Pretty darned careless of her, leaving her wallet behind. She had pulled it out to pay for gas and had never put it back into her purse. Still, it lay there on the console, unmolested.

Gaze drawn to the back seat despite her hurry, Nikki eyed not only her portfolio and boxed art supplies piled on the upholstery, but the bulging canvas totes hinting at how full the trunk was with everything else she owned. Well, everything might be an exaggeration. Most of what she'd owned had gone up in flames. This was all she had left. Nikki Sharp running? Nikki Sharp didn't run. She pretended she had someplace else to go. In this case, however, she did. The manager of Hannah's department store in the impossibly quaint town of Connor Falls, Pennsylvania, had offered her a job. A temporary one, true, but an offer a hundred and fifty miles away from her former home suited her needs to a capital "T."

Nikki backed from the car, straightening on the sidewalk, wallet clutched to her jacket front. She locked the doors with her other hand, setting the alarm, the annoying little chirp causing a passerby to jump. "Sorry," Nikki muttered. People in this town likely never alarmed their cars.

Shoving the wallet and keys into her purse, Nikki headed back to the bakery. When she got inside, the white bag awaited her, along with a cup of coffee beside it on the counter.

"I had a pot brewing in the back. Figured you could use one. It's on the house."

Nikki squeezed her eyes shut and opened them in a rapid, awkward blink. *Not the time for tears, you idiot.* "Thanks. That's…very nice of you."

"Are you all right?"

Nikki nodded. "Just tired. How much do I owe you?"

"Three bucks."

"Really?"

"Too much?"

"Goodness, not at all." Nikki retrieved her wallet from the flotsam in her purse and pulled out a five-dollar bill. While she waited for the change, she yanked the coffee cup from the counter and breathed in the delicious scent. Taking the change and the bag, she dropped both into the purse's cavernous recesses. "Yum. Smells like you put sugar and cream in here," she commented about the coffee. "How'd you know?"

"Just a guess."

"Are you…are you Gina Hart?"

The woman nodded, curiosity seeping into her amused expression.

Nikki moved the coffee beneath her chin, where she could still smell the contents and feel the heat. "I'm supposed to talk to you. I'm Nikki Sharp. I'm not sure if anyone mentioned me to you, but I was told to speak with you about a place for rent short-term. The one I thought I had engaged fell through yesterday, but the person with the apartment said you would know of another place available."

Gina Hart's brows shot up. She jerked a finger at her. "You're the one from Brewster?"

"I am the one from Brewster," Nikki said.

"You're going to work for Tessa McAdams on the holiday displays."

"That's the plan. I just need a place to stay. Like I said, the apartment I had arranged to rent fell through last minute."

With a nod, Gina reached beneath the counter and slid open a drawer. A second later she had plopped an old-fashioned wire-bound address book onto the sparkling tile. Bits of paper scattered from the pages like leaves in the wind. She didn't seem troubled by their escape and tore a piece off a nearby bag in order to scrawl something across it.

"Here you go. Sheila Jefferson and her husband have been looking for a renter, short-term or otherwise. She was in here today and is waiting for you to head on over."

Gina dropped the paper onto Nikki's palm. "I can't just pop in on them, can I?" Nikki said, eyes wide. Gina laughed.

"They're expecting you. I told them you might be looking for a place when Tessa first mentioned you to me. I double-checked with Sheila today to make sure, because—well, to make sure. Wouldn't want you driving over there for nothing. I'll give them a call so they know you're on your way."

Nikki hesitated. People weren't really this nice. Usually something else was in play. Gina hadn't asked any questions, not a single one. Nikki hadn't spoken to these Jeffersons, either, and she hadn't really said yes to the whole rental situation. Not that she had much choice. Not at nearly five o'clock in the evening and a new job ready to be started the next day. "How much is the rent? Do you know?"

Gina shrugged. "You'll have to take that up with Sheila. I'm sure it'll be reasonable."

"Okay." Not much more to talk about, then. Apparently—at least in the mind of Gina Hart and perhaps even the Jeffersons—everything had already been settled. Nikki stowed the address in her coat pocket. "Thank you. Thank you for your help. And the coffee." She headed for the door, pausing with a hand on the knob. She glanced back at Gina.

Gina jerked her chin. "That way. Straight out of town. Take your first left after the white church and the next right."

How did the woman do that? First the coffee, now the directions without a question or word uttered. Good with people, Nikki guessed. In awe and a little suspicious, she thanked Gina again and departed with the sleigh bells ringing over her head. Why did that not drive the woman crazy, listening to those bells every single time a customer entered or exited? Granted, she had been the only patron in the past fifteen minutes, but with Thanksgiving only days away dozens of people were bound to be in and out of there every hour very soon.

Or would there be? Nikki glanced up and down the quiet street as she settled behind the wheel of her car. Picturesque and decorated with an eye to tradition more than whimsy, the sidewalks of Connor Falls just prior to the holiday season seemed rather empty. Nikki studied the green wreaths hanging from old-fashioned lampposts, the twinkling lights around shop windows. The bookstore directly across the street from where she sat possessed a charming display and, while she watched, two customers went in and two more came out carrying packages. Perhaps it wasn't that the sidewalks were empty, only not as ridiculously crowded as those she'd grown used to, at any time of year.

Pulling her car from the parking spot, Nikki scanned the stores while she drove to the next corner, where she planned to circle the block to leave town in the direction Gina had indicated. All the buildings appeared to have been built around the turn of the prior century, if not before, the architectural detail stunning and in some cases quite unique. By the time Nikki got herself situated, driving back toward the north end of Main Street, she felt a little like she had fallen in love.

*　　*　　*

By the light of her headlights, Nikki checked the address written across the paper strip against the numbers on the rural mailbox. Ascertaining they were the same, she got back into her car and turned into the long, graveled driveway. When she got closer to the house, she maneuvered her car into a space next to a weathered blue pickup truck. An SUV was parked inside a red barn and beyond it sat a small front-end loader. Above the open double doors hung an enormous wreath with a huge crimson bow. The three-storey fieldstone farmhouse bore a smaller version on the front door beneath the porch overhang. Electric candles lit each window and greens wrapped the porch railing. With a little snow, Nikki mused, the place would resemble a greeting card. An early greeting card. Apparently, the Jeffersons liked to get a jump on their holiday decorations.

Yanking her keys from the ignition, Nikki spotted the front door opening. A woman in sweatshirt and jeans and black rubber boots stepped out, shoving her arms into an oversized coat. She pulled a hat onto her salt-and-pepper hair while making her way across the porch and onto the driveway. Nikki opened the car door and stepped into a chill and unexpected wind blowing across the open fields behind her.

The woman held out her hand. "Sheila Jefferson," she said in introduction. "And you must be the young lady looking for a place to rent."

"I am, indeed," said Nikki. "Nikki Sharp." She clasped Sheila's fingers, returning the woman's firm grasp. Glancing at the house behind her, Nikki wondered if the apartment might be upstairs, perhaps in a renovated attic. That would be lovely. She could almost picture it, with a peaked ceiling, gabled windows, wide plank floors and exposed stone walls. She was, of course, getting ahead of herself. She'd be happy with whatever the Jeffersons offered. She had no time for being fussy. Not only that, but the smaller and less impressive the residence, the cheaper the rent. She had to be practical. She had to be realistic. She had to accept her life had changed.

"Pete's not here at the moment," Sheila went on. "He wanted to be, just to meet you, but he's fine with the plan. Come on, I'll show you what we've got going on."

The plan? Nikki thought, following as Sheila strode with an energetic stride toward a narrow, graveled path. Nikki hurried to keep up, shoving her dangling purse back up on her shoulder. As they rounded the corner, a narrow, two-storey building came into view about forty feet away, constructed of the same multi-hued fieldstone as the main house. Two windows on the lower floor cast golden rectangles across the ground below.

"This way." Sheila pushed open a large red door on the structure's windowless side. "The fellow renovating the main house had been using it on occasion, rather than driving home after a long day of work."

"I don't want to put anyone out," Nikki said hastily. "Please, I really don't."

"Not a problem. I already spoke to him, too. I—oh, here he is! Rory, goodness, I thought you'd gone on home already."

Nikki started as a dark-haired man straightened from his crouched position on the floor, his head nearly brushing the exposed beams crossing the low ceiling overhead. The light from a nearby lamp touched a jaw shadowed by a day's growth of beard and lit dark eyes behind lowered lashes. In one arm he held a small duffel bag tucked up against his ribcage.

"Sorry, Sheila," he said. "I was just straightening up a bit in here."

Nikki stared, overcome by a sense of déjà vu. Something about the man seemed familiar, although for the life of her she couldn't figure out who he looked like or how it would even be possible. She had never been anywhere near Connor Falls before. Perhaps he resembled a client? Yet despite the vague recognition, she knew if she had met him before she wouldn't have forgotten, if only due to his unusual height. Mentally shaking herself, Nikki gave him a nod of greeting.

The man's brows lowered in a quickly vanishing frown. "Hello."

"Rory, Nikki Sharp," said Sheila. "Nikki, Rory."

Nikki reached out for his hand and shook it. "Nice to meet you," she said. "And I am sorry. I didn't know I would be upsetting anyone's routine."

"No reason to apologize," Rory said quietly. "I need to be tending to some things at home anyway."

The way he said the words 'at home' struck a strange note. Looking away with another frown, Rory brushed his sweatshirt's torn and paint-splattered sleeve across a table top. "It should be presentable in here now," he said.

"Rory, don't you worry about any of that, you hear me? Nikki and I will take care of things,"

Sheila told him.

"Thanks." He hoisted a stuffed tool bag off the floor. Nikki watched him, feeling awkward. She could tell he wasn't thrilled about her usurping his place in this little house and couldn't blame him for that. It seemed odd in retrospect that Sheila Jefferson and her husband had agreed to let her come.

Rory grabbed his coat and eased past, nodding at them both, a massive man in a small space moving without noise. At the door he paused, glancing back at Nikki as if he wanted to say something else. With the light from the lamp behind her full on his face, she realized his eyes weren't quite as dark as she'd thought them. Not black at all, but a deep, deep blue, shadowed by thick lashes. She met his gaze, wondering again if they'd met before. Nonsense, that. Even if her memory was faulty, he behaved as one would with a stranger. It would come to her later, some resemblance to a client or shop owner in Brewster. Just a déjà vu type moment.

The latch fell softly into place behind his retreating form. Nikki turned to find Sheila watching her.

"You all right?" she asked. "You mustn't fret about him. He really did need to be getting home."

An odd thing to say, Nikki mused, forcing the corners of her mouth upward. "If you say so."

"I do," Sheila answered. "Trust me. Let me just show you around. We'll get some fresh bedding in here for you, and some towels. I'll give you directions to the supermarket, too, for tomorrow.

Pete and I, we lived in this place for a stretch while parts of the main house were being made livable—again—so it has all the amenities, even if it isn't quite the most fashionable home you've ever seen."

Following her around the tiny building, Nikki noted how much the summer kitchen/cottage resembled what it must have been originally. Though minimal, the updating for function and comfort was perfect. "I think it's beautiful."

Sheila arched her brows. "Really? Well, that's a surprise, it truly is. Not a lot of folks see it that way. Rory, now, he has an eye for old buildings like this one. Oh, and it gets cold in here. I guess you can feel that already? There's a cord of wood right beside the building for the fireplace. You just keep it stoked up as high as you like."

Nikki peered out the window in the direction Sheila pointed, locating a lean-to filled with wood. "Thank you. For everything. Your kindness is more than I could have hoped for. You don't even know me."

"Don't need to. We know Gina very well, and Tessa is her friend. Neither one of them seemed to think we had any reason to worry about you."

"Oh, you don't," Nikki assured her. "And I'll pay you straightaway for the rent, as soon as you let me know how much it is." Even as she said the words, she knew she should have had this discussion in advance, but she didn't expect these people were out for a killing. Whatever they asked would be worth it.

"We'll discuss that tomorrow and come to some sort of meeting of the minds. In the meantime, let's run over to the house and get those things you'll need, all right?"

A short time later, Nikki had made up the bed with fresh sheets. Fluffy towels hung in the bathroom, and a turkey and cheese sandwich had been supplied by Sheila. After several trips to cart in everything from the car, Nikki lowered herself into the only chair in the living room—a canvas camp chair more comfortable than it looked—and took a bite from the sandwich, chewing slowly as she contemplated events.

Connor Falls seemed as good a place as any to hide out for a bit while she sorted out what to do next. Maybe even better than most. Something about the easy attitude of the people she had met so far appealed to her. The fact she had a job for which she'd soon be paid came as an added benefit.

Closing her eyes, she leaned back in the camp chair, enjoying the fire's warmth and the distinct dressing Sheila had spread across the turkey. She took another blind bite, lowering the sandwich to the paper plate in her lap. The flames crackled, logs shifted, and a faint woodsmoke scent wafted momentarily around the room as a rising wind howled across the chimney top. A sudden shiver danced along Nikki's spine, spreading right out to her fingertips. She sat up, almost dislodging the meal's remains from her lap.

The building fire had seemed the final straw in events conspiring against her. And yet, that was believed an accident on someone's part in one of the other apartments. No one was to blame, and certainly nothing in the universe was singling her out for trouble. For a while, though, it had felt that way. Right up to the day she had answered the call from Tessa McAdams. A fortuitous and welcome call. Nikki had quickly made up her mind to take the job Tessa offered. Connor Falls could be just the place for her bruised soul to heal.

Then again, she might be hoping for a bit too much.

Rising, Nikki turned her back to the flames on the hearth while she consumed the final bites from her sandwich. She sighed as the heat baked the tension from her muscles. After rolling her neck a few times, she tossed another log onto the fire and plugged her cell phone in to charge, before heading for the narrow stairs and an early bed. At the staircase, Nikki's gaze fell on two books lying on their side in an otherwise tidy bookcase. Walking over, she took them out, wondering if Rory had accidently left them behind. She pegged him an uncomplicated sort, the type who liked to read about tools of his trade or perhaps the latest novel by a favorite male author. On the first count she was right, since the book on top dealt with 18th century architecture. Made sense, considering what he did here at the Jefferson home. She would have liked to read that one herself, but if it did belong to him, she felt funny taking it without asking. As for the second…

Nikki chewed her lower lip, staring at the book's cover, a self-help book addressing ways to deal with loss. Her mind shied away from the way it felt, this voyeuristic peek into an intimate portion of a stranger's life. Then again, she reminded herself, the books could easily belong to the Jeffersons. Sheila had said they'd been staying in the cottage for a time. Nikki returned the books to the shelf and climbed the stairs. She shirked her clothes off in the tiny room and buried herself deep beneath the laundry-fresh covers on the old, narrow bed.

Tomorrow, she would get up bright and early and start the next few days in her life. This was the way she'd been doing it. Life. A day or two, a week at a time. Bite-sized chunks. Because reaching out for more left too many pitfalls in the way.

Chapter Two

Opening her eyes, Nikki stared up at sunlight reflecting along massive wooden beams, unable, for a moment, to remember where she was. When the previous day's events came skipping back into her sleep-addled brain, air rushed in release from her nose and she sat up.

"Brrr!"

She had better get more wood onto that fire, and fast. Wrapping the down comforter around her shoulders, she hopped out of bed and shoved her bare feet into the boots she'd left on the floor beneath the window. At the sound of a metal door closing, she looked out toward the driveway and the blue pickup backed in beside her car. Rory stood at the pickup's bed, a five-gallon bucket of paint hitched up onto his shoulder. A nighttime fall of snow spattered the gravel and the leaves of the trimmed evergreens next to the barn.

Rory's head turned. She started to back away,

but instead raised her hand in greeting. Ignoring her, he pivoted with a shift of the bucket and walked toward the front of Sheila's house. Nikki stepped back from the glass. Likely, the sun on the panes had prevented him seeing her.

Dismissing the incident, she went to add wood to the fire, finding it had died to embers. She decided to skip the wood. The propane heater set into the wall would keep the pipes from freezing. Sheila had told her so. They kept it at fifty-two degrees during the colder months for that purpose. The fire happened to be an added bonus to avoid hypothermia. When she came back from her meeting with Tessa at Hannah's, she'd build another fire.

Following the fastest shower of her life, Nikki hastened into her clothes and prepared a short list of items to pick up at the grocery store on her way home. The refrigerator was one of those dormitory units and wouldn't hold much. She wanted to stop by the bookstore, too, for a magazine or two. Except for the lack of a weather report, Nikki had no objection to the absence of television. Peace and quiet was exactly what she needed.

Portfolio in hand, Nikki strolled out to her car and slipped her fingers beneath the driver door handle as Rory appeared at the back of his truck, reaching inside for something else. She hadn't even heard him coming. "Hi," she said, loudly enough for him to hear her. She stood with her door open, waiting.

Lifting his head, he continued to shift things around in the truck bed. He nodded. "Morning."

"Look, Rory, right? I'm really sorry if I've inconvenienced you with all of this. I had no idea."

He straightened, swinging the long handle of a huge sledge hammer across his shoulder with a flick of the wrist. "No reason you would, being a stranger to Connor Falls and all. Sheila's not wrong. I needed to go home."

I needed to go home. Nikki had a flash of the self-help book and pushed it away. Not her business. "Okay. I won't mention it again."

"How long are you staying?"

"Through the holidays." She slipped her portfolio behind the seat and tossed her purse beside it. "That's the plan, at any rate."

He nodded once more, his expression changing, an alteration in his eyes too quick to follow. He ran his hand through his short-cropped dark hair. He hadn't shaved, his beard grown in a little fuller. "Enjoy your day."

Nikki bit her tongue on another apology. She wrestled with guilt every day. She couldn't let something she hadn't known about be her undoing.

Sliding into the driver's seat, Nikki watched him walk to the front door of Sheila's home. He paused to remove the sledge hammer from his shoulder before ducking his head to walk inside, tan coat stretching across broad shoulders, product, she figured, of genetics and hard labor rather than a weight bench at a gym. She considered the extra few pounds she had put on recently. Maybe she should take up a bit of laboring.

* * *

Rory opened the door again, deciding he had to say something. He had to. Catching the vivid flash of her brake lights as she turned the car out of the driveway, he slowly shut the door, lowering the latch into place. His gaze shifted to his left, to the sledge hammer leaning against the wall in the corner. He hadn't even needed the damned thing. It had been an excuse to go back out there. And he'd said nothing.

She didn't remember him. He'd thought for a moment when she'd met his eyes last night that she did. How would she even put two and two together when he had been introduced to her that evening so long ago by his first name, not as Rory? Besides, his appearance here was so out of context with that other time, three years past and miles away, as to be some other life entirely. It had been a shock realizing he knew the woman Sheila brought into the cottage last night, but he thought he had recovered well. At least he hoped so, because if he never got up the nerve to remind Nikki of that evening, then he didn't want her finding out at all.

She had changed, sure, but not all that much. He knew the same could not be said of him. Even people who saw him every day said so. He couldn't help it. Grief had a way of altering everything from attitude to physical appearance. And the jeans and paint-stained sweatshirt she'd seen him in the night before were far removed from the suit he'd been wearing at the holiday party in Manhattan. Which was fine, because he didn't want her to think he expected any sort of social nicety because of that brief association. But the coincidence of them being in the same place at the same time again bothered him, like he shouldn't let it go unremarked.

Shaking his head, Rory strode to the back of the house, where he had already spread a tarp across the floor and laid out the rolling pan and roller preparing to give the walls a fresh coat of paint. Taking out a screwdriver, he popped open the five-gallon container, giving a quick stir to the contents with a splattered yard stick. He poured a little paint into the pan, catching the drips with a rag he tossed down afterward onto some old newspapers. As he straightened, a spark of sunlight through the window caught his eye and he turned.

Kat loved the snow. Each winter since came filled with reminders he'd thought in time would lose their potency. He had stopped celebrating Christmas that unbearable year, except quietly and alone, without fanfare, without company, without real joy.

A brilliant red cardinal alighted on the snowy branch and, for the first time since Kat's passing, Rory itched for his camera in his hands. If he still sent out holiday cards, the scene would have been one of clichéd but perfect winter enchantment.

No point in that. Not anymore.

Pushing the roller through the paint in the pan, he began the day's work.

*   *   *

On her way to the manager's office, Nikki checked out the department store. From the outside,

Hannah's still bore the solid, stone imprint of its beginnings, but inside it had been modernized. Nikki had taken a few minutes after parking her car to peruse the windows, too. Tessa had told her the employees had pulled some of the stored decorations from the basement, put them in place, tried to spruce up the look of the products in the windows for the holidays, but with the abrupt resignation of their window dresser—visual merchandiser, Nikki had said to the woman, before she could stop herself—Tessa desperately needed a replacement. This year, more than any other, the windows had to be perfect. The department store was celebrating its one-hundredth anniversary. Tessa had been pleased as rum sauce to get Nikki so quickly and Nikki had been equally as delighted to have the opportunity. Her getaway would have been funded by savings alone otherwise. At least now she had an income and a purpose.

Outside the manager's door, Nikki knocked, hiking the portfolio up under her arm. Hearing Tessa's voice calling her inside, she entered, startled to find the small office filled with people. A woman with strawberry blond hair stood up from behind the desk.

"Nikki?"

Nikki nodded. "Yes."

"Come in! It's so nice to meet you in person. I'm Tessa McAdams, if you hadn't figured that out already. Everybody, this is Nikki Sharp. Nikki, this is everybody. Chamber of Commerce members mostly. Sorry about cramming everyone in here. There's a school board meeting taking place at the town hall today."

Nikki glanced around, doing her best to smile. She recognized one face and her teeth-baring broke into a genuine grin. Gina Hart waved from the corner by the window. No wonder the woman had been so keen to be helpful. She knew why Nikki had come.

Tessa skirted her desk and came out to meet Nikki in the center of the office. She led Nikki to an empty table against the wall. "We're all anxious to see what you've drafted for our consideration. I know, I know, you didn't have the specs, but I'm sure you've created some beautiful suggestions." Tessa turned back to the gathering. "You've all seen the photos I've sent you of Nikki's prior work, yes?" Murmured assents met her question. She turned back to Nikki. "Let's see what you have for our town."

Nikki had made presentations like this many times before, but for some reason her fingers shook as she reached for the zipper on the case. Tessa stepped aside to give Nikki room to display her renderings across the tabletop. In the ten years she had been designing modern, breathtaking window displays, she had never anticipated a customer's dissatisfaction and had never been disappointed. Tessa had found Nikki based on word of mouth and the endorsements and slideshows portfolios on her website. None were exaggerated. She really was good at her job. But as Nikki lay each illustration side by side, knowing she had every reason to be proud of her work, something told her the designs were not what these townsfolk had come expecting to see.

Heart slipping into her stomach, Nikki backed away from the drawings, fighting the urge to run from the room. She had always been a professional and a lucky one at that. Everyone had failures. She just didn't want one now.

With a modest nod, Nikki walked to the other side of the room, giving Tessa and the business owners time to review the design portfolio. A dozen men and women crowded the table. Nikki shut out their quiet discussions, spinning to study an aerial view of the nearest buildings from the third-floor window of Tessa's office. Gina joined her a moment later.

"They're beautiful," Gina whispered.

"The buildings? Yes, they are."

"I was talking about your designs."

"But…" Nikki said.

"There isn't a 'but'."

"I can hear one, Gina. I have this gut feeling I haven't grasped what Tessa expected, let alone the rest of you. Why are you all here, by the way? I thought I was only doing Hannah's windows."

Gina shifted around, easing her hips down onto the window ledge. "I think we're trying to get an idea for a little cohesion for the rest of Main Street. A little late, I know. And what is your gut telling you, by the way?"

"That I needed to capture the heart of the town, and I haven't."

Gina nodded—a striking woman, Gina Hart, with her black hair and tea-colored eyes, her confident stance, her place among the community.

Nikki envied her. Except for her art, Nikki often experienced a distinct lack of confidence in many situations. She put on a good show, but her heart knew better.

Still, she was a professional. She needed to get on with acting like one.

Nikki turned to face the room. She could tell by their expressions they hadn't connected with the presentation. Nikki decided to head them off at the pass.

"I appreciate the time you all took in reviewing what I had prepared. However, since coming to Connor Falls last night, I have quite a different impression of the…flavor of your community. I can see you are all too polite to admit to being less than enthusiastic about what you've been shown."

Several people began to speak, but their protestations tapered off at Nikki's look.

"They really are lovely," Gina said behind her.

Nikki smiled. "I would ask that you give me until tomorrow to come up with a better plan for Hannah's windows. One you can all get behind, one that will engage and whose elements can be used in each of your windows. Is that all right with you?"

For several seconds no one said anything, and then Tessa spoke. "You're right. Although stunning, they weren't quite what I had expected. Too…I don't know. Glitzy? That might not be the right term. But we're a small town and quite proud of that fact."

"I can see that," Nikki said. "I don't think I quite understood how much from our conversations and I apologize."

Tessa shrugged. "I have no problem with giving you a couple of days, if you need it."

"Thanksgiving is coming soon. I think I should try to get the new sketches to you all by tomorrow."

With a smile, Tessa nodded. "I trust you to bring something fantastic to the table. Are the rest of you available to come back to another meeting?"

After a brief discussion, the group came to a unanimous agreement to meet again briefly the following afternoon at two o'clock. Nikki gathered up her drawings as the members filed out. It should have been obvious to her these wouldn't suit. What had she been thinking?

"Thank you."

Nikki spun around to face Tessa. "I haven't done anything yet."

"No, but you're willing to get it right."

Nikki zipped the portfolio shut. "You're paying me to get it right, Tessa. I won't do anything less."

"Nikki…"

"I'm sorry, was that too candid? But it's true. Just like you're proud of your town, I'm proud of the work I do. I want to make sure I meet your needs." Nikki grasped the handle of the case against her waist.

"Everything of yours that I have seen has looked like a labor of love, not merely meeting a client's needs but exceeding them. And you're right, I didn't quite see that in this presentation. Walk around town, get a deeper feel for it, see if you can understand what it means to be a part of this community. I think it will help you."

"You're right. Of course, you are." Nikki

started moving toward the door.

"We celebrate Christmas in a traditional manner here in Connor Falls, but we want to show we aren't mired in old habits."

"Understood."

"You'll do it, Nikki. I have a good feeling about you."

Nikki thanked her again and left. Quickly, before the woman noted the moisture in her eyes. Out on the street, she decided to start straightaway and returned the portfolio to her car, taking her sketch book with her instead for her walk through the town. She'd barely gone half a block when someone called her name. Nikki glanced over her shoulder. "Gina! Hi."

She waited while Gina caught up to her. "That wasn't too bad in there, was it?" the woman asked.

Nikki shook her head. "I realized rather quickly that what I had prepared wouldn't work here."

"Good thing you have a whole day to totally re-do it all." Gina smiled in commiseration.

Nikki responded to Gina's friendly manner with a self-effacing laugh. "I can cram two weeks' work into a single night if I must. With plenty of coffee. Not a problem."

Gina's grin widened. "That's the spirit. How are you liking your place at the Jeffersons?"

"It's a sweet little house," Nikka said. "Very cozy. I feel bad, though."

"Why?"

"There was a man staying there. Rory—"

"Ah," said Gina. "Don't you worry about him. That was only for convenience. He'll work it out."

He'll work it out. What an odd thing to be said about him, yet again. Still, being exonerated for the second time for the man's exodus from the Jefferson's little place—the first being from Sheila Jefferson—Nikki decided she really should just shrug it off. At least for now. Nikki would apologize to him if she ran into him again.

With another smile and a wave, Gina hurried back to her bakery, leaving Nikki standing on the corner trying to decide which way to go first. She headed down a side street, where the early decorators had draped greenery on fences, affixed wreaths to doors. Single electric candles burned behind window glass, still on and visible beneath a clouded sky. She walked past a small, picturesque white church and took several photos with her phone. She took pictures, too, of the Victorian architecture, then strode the Main Street she had only viewed briefly the day before, studying the various storefronts, window shapes, the items already displayed. The buildings had been constructed at least a century ago. People strolled and paused and went in and out of the various shops without hurry even on this wintry day.

The words *what's next* popped into Nikki's brain, the way they'd been doing for days.

What's next. What's next.

Like some annoying throaty little bird.

The *what's next* kept her thinking she might never go back to the familiar, the once-comfortable. But she couldn't stay here, either. Everything was temporary.

What's next.

Yes, temporary. She really needed to strike that attitude from her mind and act as if it were permanent. Get the job done. Do it right.

Nikki returned to Hannah's to study the huge, stone block edifice. She'd viewed the images Tessa had emailed her and used them to make her illustrations. However, she hadn't had the feel for the town at that time. Now, she did. After making a few quick sketches and taking several more photographs, she headed back to her car, intending to stop at a grocery store and then return to the little cottage with nourishment and a plan.

On her way down the main street, she passed Connor Falls Book Emporium again. Her practiced eye went to the window, picturing it in full Christmas display. She quickly pulled into another parking space, deciding she should also purchase something to read during the long evening hours without television, or any other interaction. Something she could drowse over before the warm fire and not worry about losing her momentum.

Entering the store, she headed over to the magazine rack. The young man behind the counter glanced up.

"Can I help you find something?" he asked.

Yes, she thought. My life.

"I'm just looking," she said, moving past the magazines to the next aisle where she'd spotted a section with a bright yellow 'local authors' sign hanging from the ceiling above. "How local are these authors?" she called as she stood in amazement of the amount of outward facing books lining the three shelves.

"Most of them live in the county," he answered. "Some are from neighboring counties."

Tipping her head to the side, she studied the covers, noting an assortment from romance and mysteries and ghost tales to volumes on area history and several titles of the coffee table variety. Enchanted by the photograph on one, she pulled the book off the shelf. The volume was titled, simply, *Home*, and the cover held a rather ethereal and beautifully framed black and white shot of a lovely, pale-haired woman crouching in a garden with a watering can, tending to the tender plants sprouting from the earth.

Nikki flipped through several pages, recognizing photographs from Connor Falls' Main Street, while others, like the cover, seemed much more personal. Nevertheless, a thread of intimacy and delicate balance bound them all together as one, cohesive subject.

Home. She smiled.

"I'll take this," she said without hesitation, marching up to the counter clutching the book against her breast. She released it to the clerk, who rang it up and slipped the volume into a shopping bag. Thanking him again, she left the store.

Back at the Jeffersons, Nikki pulled into the space beside Rory's pickup. Striding past the house to the cottage door, she wondered what he might be doing in the main house. Painting, she supposed, based on the large container she'd seen him carrying in. But what the heck had the sledgehammer been for?

After putting all but the salad for her lunch

away in the single cabinet and tiny refrigerator, Nikki went back outside to collect an armload of wood so she could rebuild the fire. Crouching low, she balanced four logs on her left arm and stood to turn. When she did, she caught sight of Rory through a window. Based on his movements, he seemed to be running a paint roller up and down the plaster walls. The exertion must have warmed him, because he'd removed the paint-splotched sweatshirt he'd worn the night before, and wore only a black tee shirt. A holey black tee shirt that clung to his broad chest and wrapped around the muscles in his upper arms. Nikki blushed crimson when he spotted her staring.

Lowering the paint roller he waved, just a slight flip of his hand, and returned to work. Nikki hurried inside. She dumped the logs into the metal basket and set several on the grate, her cheeks still burning. Following several unsuccessful attempts, Nikki finally got the fire going. Retrieving the salad, she set it on the metal tray table and picked up her new book before settling into the camp chair near the hearth. Forking romaine and various additions into her mouth, she opened the book across her lap, turning the pages one at a time, exposing the photographer's world, his ideals, to her eye. About halfway through the book, she decided to return to the introduction, hoping for further insight. Finding herself at the dedication instead, she gazed down at the words for a long time, the next forkful of salad forgotten in her hand.

To Kat, my wife, my inspiration, my home.

Tears stung her eyes. She blinked them away,

shutting the book with a finger still inside to hold her page as she looked for the name of the man who possessed such sentiments. When she found it, her moist eyes slowly widened. Robert R. Hollis. Robert R. Hollis, she repeated in her head. She knew that name. How did she know that name?

Setting her fork on her plate, Nikki used both hands to find the author page. There, beneath a photo of the man, the caption read: "Robert Roderick Hollis, Rory to his friends and neighbors in his home town of Connor Falls, Pennsylvania." She stared at the photo for several minutes before closing the book and setting it aside. Standing, she grabbed her coat from the nearby hook on the wall and slipped her arms into it, pulled the zipper up to her chin. Retrieving the volume from the floor, Nikki headed over to the main house.

Chapter Three

Rory caught a peripheral glimpse of someone passing the window. He lowered the roller into the pan and leaned onto his knuckles on the sill, peering out in time to see Nikki Sharp tromping around the corner. A few seconds later, he heard her knock on the back door. Resigned, he wiped his hands on a rag and went to open it.

"Hi—"

Nikki ducked under his arm and stepped onto the tarp. He shut the door and turned to face her.

"Why didn't you come to the front door?" he asked.

"Because I didn't want you to have to stop what you were doing to let me in," Nikki said. "And I guess that makes no sense, because you just had to do that anyway."

"I did," he agreed.

She took a deep breath, expanding her coat against the book she held clutched in her crossed arms.

"Did you need something?" he asked. Patiently, considering he had a wet paint roller drying in the pan.

She looked at him in silence, gnawing her lower lip. After a moment she unfolded her arms and held the book out toward him, cover first. He groaned inwardly.

"I know you," she said.

"Yes."

"Why did I not recognize you?"

"I've changed."

"Not that much. Not really. Not now that I know. You never mentioned you were a photographer."

"Because I wasn't," he said. "Not then. I'd given it up."

Looking around for a place to sit, Nikki lowered herself onto a step ladder, setting her booted feet onto the bottom rung. She held his book in her lap, head bowed, staring at it.

"Why?" she asked. "Why did you give up taking these wonderful photographs?"

His heart clenched in his chest. "I don't want to talk about it." He bent for the roller, returned to the wet edge on the wall beside her. Paint spreading over plaster was the only noise in the quiet until she shifted on her perch. The ladder creaked.

"Did you recognize me?" she asked.

"Yes."

"Why didn't you say anything?"

"I thought it would be better not to."

"For what reason?"

He pivoted to face her with the roller in his hand. "Because this degree of coincidence makes me very uncomfortable." Like fate, he wanted to add. And he had no faith in fate's whims.

Nikki bit her lip again, strumming the book's edge with her index finger. "I don't remember you telling me you were married, either."

"Did it matter?" he countered, another pinch to his heart. "We were only talking, you and I."

"I know. It's just…the dedication in this book is so lovely. I would have thought she might have been the first thing you mentioned, your wife. But in that whole five hours, you said nothing."

Five hours. Like she'd committed the evening to permanent memory. Moving to the window, he curved his free hand around the deep frame, lowering the other against his thigh, the paint roller in it pointed toward the sky outside. Staring out at the grounds, Rory inhaled and released a ragged breath. "Please," he said. "I would ask you to stop. I…I don't want to answer any more questions." He stood silently for several memory-staggered heartbeats of his own, memories from that very evening, an evening he had not forgotten either but for reasons which had to be quite different from hers.

Making a small, sudden noise, she shifted her weight again on the ladder. "You just rolled paint down your jeans."

"I—" He glanced down. "Crap."

She appeared beside him with the rag he'd left on the floor. "Here."

"Thanks."

As he dabbed at the blobbed paint on already spattered denim, he saw her test the windowsill with her finger. Finding it hadn't been painted yet, she scooted back onto the deep sill and turned her head to gaze outside. The soft light touched her face, her one shoulder, the hands clasped in her lap, shadowing the rest of her dramatically. For the second time that day, he longed for his camera. Pushing the yearning away, he strode across the room and tossed the rag down.

"Was there anything else?" he asked. "I really should get back to work."

From the windowsill came marked silence. Rory glanced over his shoulder. Nikki sat with her mouth open, expression stunned, yet quickly collected herself and pushed off the sill, marching over to collect her book from the ladder.

"I'm sorry," he said. "That seemed rude. I didn't mean it to be."

"I know. It's fine. You have work to do."

"I'm sorry," he said again, wondering why the heck he felt the need to continue apologizing.

"You don't have to say keep saying that. I really do understand. I have work to do, too, believe it or not." She headed toward the door.

"Nikki."

Her name felt strange on his lips, too familiar despite having used it all those months and months ago, making him feel stripped raw, like his skin was on inside-out, every nerve ending exposed and burned and vulnerable.

She paused with her hand on the door knob. "Yes?"

"We'll talk, okay? When I have more time. It would be nice to catch up." Catch up. As if they'd ever actually been friends. They'd spent two hours at a dull party in each other's company, and several more at the small bar downstairs. But he hadn't forgotten. That meant something, and knowing made his stomach perform strange acrobatics in his gut. He almost wished he hadn't spoken just now, had let her walk out the door without any promises.

"Okay," she said. "You let me know."

She left. Nothing in the way she uttered those words, moved, closed the door, strolled past the window toward the cottage, gave him any clue whether he'd pissed her off or she expected him to come through. He went back to work, but painting's monotony didn't stop him from recalling the vibrant woman in the sleek sheath dress who'd had a way of making him laugh at an obligatory party miles and miles from the home where, only months earlier, his wife had passed away. He had hated himself for it then, and still did.

*　　*　　*

Nikki walked into the house and shut the door. Perhaps a little more forcefully than she had intended. Feeling foolish, she opened the door again and closed it with a quiet push. Not that it made any difference except in her own head.

She tossed the book onto the small counter and returned to the fire, where her unfinished salad awaited her. Shoveling in the plate's contents, she thought about the recent conversation. His final dismissive tone had irked her more than anything. After all, she'd only been looking to tell him she remembered him. Perhaps, also to express shock over the circumstances. She would never have expected to run into him again.

She'd never gotten that far, of course. He had seemed most uncomfortable with her presence. She couldn't understand why. Like he said, the remembered evening had been nothing but talk. Enjoyable conversation, yes, but no more than that. He hadn't cheated on his wife, hadn't made any hints he looked for something more. Nothing even close to putting such an idea into the man's mind, or hers. He'd been funny, brought out her own humor. She remembered now they had both laughed so hard they complained about aching stomach muscles. No looks, no innuendo, not even physical proximity. Just fun.

He didn't seem so much fun anymore. Something had happened.

"Oh."

Recalling the self-help book on the shelf, Nikki slowly lowered the fork from her mouth. The loss referenced in that book's title had been his.

His wife, his inspiration, his home.

Oh God.

Such tragedy would certainly explain why he'd turned his back on photography, although he'd just told her he had given it up before Nikki met him. Had his wife already passed by that time? Or had hers been a long illness?

Nikki fought the urge to run back over to the house, seek confirmation and then tell him how sorry she was for dredging up something so painful. Staring into the flames, she thought about things like guilt and shame and sorrow. No wonder he'd wanted her gone as fast as possible.

Rising, she scraped the sparse salad remnants into the trash pail and placed the dish in the tiny sink. Retrieving Rory's book, she once more opened it across her lap and spent a long time studying each photo, her perspective altered by Rory's loss. Linking the tiny clues, things made sense. The photographs displayed his love for the town, and more obviously for his wife. Following various winter scenes, the very last photo was a close-up of a feminine hand—Kat's, she felt sure—cupping an ornament on an evergreen branch. She might have been removing it, or just balancing the lovely silver bell in place. The other branches stood empty, the lone ornament's reflective surface revealing the woman and the room behind. Every photo in Rory's book captured something timeless, as if to give homage to very precise moments, as if...

As if he knew it would all be changing forever.

Nausea rolled in Nikki's stomach. She wondered how someone dealt with such perspective-altering knowledge, changing everything that came before, everything to come after. She could do nothing to help him, of course. She knew that. Compassion from a near-stranger, especially at this juncture and from someone he didn't want to remember, wouldn't help him at all.

All this was based on assumption, too. She had to remember that, not fly off feeling guilty and remorseful. She'd find out the truth, though. Sheila Jefferson would know.

Nikki set Rory's book aside and broke out her sketchbook. She needed to get moving on these designs, and fast. The finals had to be ready before tomorrow's scheduled meeting. With Thanksgiving a week away, the crunch was on. When Nikki had taken the job, she'd recognized the limited timeframe for completion, and had been a bit too numbed by recent events in her life to be daunted. Now, she fought down panic.

These things were usually planned out months, if not a whole year in advance. Hannah's prior "window dresser" had dropped the ball, for sure. She'd been engaged more in her upcoming nuptials than getting everything ready for the Christmas display. The fact the woman had quit and moved to another state with her husband following the wedding hadn't helped matters. Tessa had supplied Nikki with the half-planned drawings and sketches together with photos of items they kept stored in the basement and often reused, in case they would help. Mostly, they hadn't. Which suited Nikki just fine. She had worked up her own ideas. But now she'd been forced to come up with new designs, new sketches and obtain everything needed to execute them in record time.

Grumbling, she set to work with laptop as well as paper and ink, recognizing evening had fallen only when she looked around and found the room beyond the single lamp at her elbow had grown shadowed. She rose, stretched, strode to the window, and peered out at the star-filled sky. The town's illumination was a mere glimmer in the distance beyond the trees. Across the field where a hill hunkered in darkness, pinpoint lights flickered in and out as a car meandered down a road through the woods. Connor Falls was a lovely area, free of the hustle she'd been used to. A haven for the moment, despite the pressure to get her job completed. It would be nice to stick around through the holidays. She had nowhere else she felt inclined to go.

Movement over by the barn caught her eye. Recognizing Rory's figure as he loaded some things into his truck bed, Nikki stepped back, not wanting to be caught watching him. Yet watching him she was, and continued to do, her brow creased by a frown.

It would be difficult to avoid him the remainder of her time here in Connor Falls, but he was so desperately uncomfortable in her presence. She hadn't quite believed him about the whole 'catching up' thing. The offer had seemed forced, a courtesy, surely not heartfelt. They had no reason to do so, anyway, nothing that needed catching up on. And yet…

And yet she felt drawn to him. Perhaps, because of his pain. Hers couldn't compare in any way to his, but she could commiserate from her own perspective about loss and heartache. She wouldn't, though. Couldn't, had no plans to. If she hadn't realized she knew him, hadn't deduced his story, she would have been sitting in this house without a thought for him. Somehow the idea of that, of not caring about what happened to another human being, made her exceedingly sad.

Still, she pushed Rory determinedly from her mind and returned to her work.

Chapter Four

Wrapped in a thick, plaid blanket, Rory got up off the couch and walked to the window. He stared out at the moon's shimmer across the frozen landscape. Somewhere out there between the work day's end and unlocking his front door, he'd felt a shift in his perspective. Those closest to him understood his issues and permitted him a margin of error in his day-to-day dealings. He often wished they wouldn't, because they made it too easy for him. As to the others, people he dealt with on a business level, at a store, in the streets, he treated them with civility and without any true connection. But today…today he had dismissed someone's feelings who deserved better, and though he knew he shouldn't trouble himself overmuch about what had happened, the momentary dismay in Nikki's expression had breached the cocooning barrier between him and life and into which he had burrowed deep.

It hurt still, no denying that. The pain was like a constant, embedded splinter he couldn't manage to remove.

He tried to remember the last time he'd recognized his abominable lack in social situations, even cared. Surely, before Kat had died. By the time he'd met Nikki, he'd already been a bear in hibernation for too long, and yet what she had given him in that relatively small timeframe was recognition he had not died, too.

It hadn't mattered. He hadn't been ready for guilt-free living. He still wasn't.

Turning from the window, he took in the couch with its twisted sheets, the lumpy pillows driven against the arm. He couldn't remember what the firm mattress on the bed felt like. Even at the cottage he slept curled in his sleeping bag. Upstairs in the home he'd shared with his wife their marriage bed stood empty and cold and bare. His sister had removed the sheets for washing long ago and he'd never bothered to replace them.

Pulling the blanket a little closer about his body, Rory headed for the stairs. At the door to the bedroom, he hesitated before reaching for the knob, grabbed it, pushed the door open. Moonlight puddled the room, pouring liquid silver over the hardwood floors, making inky shadows from the furnishings, glittering edges delineating nothing he would have recognized by day. The mattress lay white and barren as a snowdrift on the four-post bed.

Walking toward the window, drawn to the night, its cold beauty, he heard the grandfather clock downstairs signaling the hour. All too soon, the sun would rise. It wouldn't be the first day he'd faced without sleep, and likely wouldn't be the last.

*   *   *

The space where Rory usually parked his truck stood empty. His absence sent a small worry scurrying through Nikki's mind, quickly dismissed. The time was barely past one. He could be at lunch, could be at the store, could be finished for the day, although the last did not seem likely. She reminded herself she hadn't chased him from his work, a place where he felt comfortable, although she had chased him from the cottage. Not deliberately. His job, the painting and whatever else he had to do, still awaited him whether she resided in the former summer kitchen or not.

Nikki slipped the portfolio with her reworked designs into her car's back seat. After climbing behind the wheel, she glanced back at it and crossed her fingers, closed her eyes, and uttered a short wish for success. At around midnight, she'd been struck by overwhelming inspiration, which had caused her to work until three in the morning altering the designs she'd already thought finished one last time.

Driving into town, Nikki passed Rory's truck coming in the opposite direction, no doubt heading to the Jefferson's farm. She lifted her hand and waved. No point in being unfriendly. He released his fingers from the wheel in a brief greeting, his expression impassive, and drove on without looking at her. Fine. That worked, too.

In town, Nikki found a space a block away from Hannah's, pulled in. She sat for several minutes eyeing the buildings along the street. What would it be like to make a place such as this home? Nothing existed to draw her back to Brewster. She hadn't been raised there, had only moved to the town with her boyfriend and stayed on after he left for another job. And another woman. But after all this time, that was neither here nor there. Although she'd settled into her life in New York, it hadn't felt like home. Nowhere did, really. As a child, she'd moved around so many times, experiencing so many schools, the loss of so many friends due to distance, she felt like a pine tree, rather than an oak—her roots spread out to keep her stable, rather than going deep.

Gathering her things, she headed into Hannah's. Early for the meeting, she went upstairs to the offices anyway. The small waiting area would be the perfect place to sit and gather her thoughts before heading inside. Instead, she met Gina as soon as she stepped from the elevator.

"Nikki, hi!"

"Hi, Gina. I know I'm early. I figured I'd sit over there for a bit and wait."

Gina walked over to the chairs with her. "I know whatever you've come up with will be perfect."

"What makes you so sure?"

"Yesterday you seemed a little uncertain. Today, you look like you're ready to go."

"Really?"

Gina nodded, smiling. "Plus, you've got talent.

We all saw that yesterday. It just wasn't exactly—"

"—right for the store and the town," Nikki finished for her. "I know. I recognized that straightaway when I pulled the designs out from my portfolio. By then, it was too late. I'm just glad to have the chance to prove myself again."

"Absolutely. Do you want a coffee or something?"

Nikki shook her head.

"Okay. I'm heading back in. We're only waiting for a couple more, so we might even start earlier than two, if that's all right?"

"That would be fine," Nikki said, and took a seat. Gina strode away toward Tessa's office. Nikki turned her head to the window, stared out across the rooftops, the portfolio and her laptop held across her lap. Something about this place, about the welcome she'd received, the friendliness of its residents so far, brought a warmth to her she hadn't experienced in quite a while.

The elevator opened again. Nikki glanced over, saw a pair she recognized from the meeting the day before but whose names she couldn't remember. She gave them a nod and a smile and watched them knock before entering at Tessa's door. Five minutes later the door opened again and Tessa herself came out, waving Nikki inside.

Nikki rose, pretended to get a better grip on the portfolio while she drew a deep breath, and then followed her into the office.

"Hi, everyone," Nikki said as she walked in and set her case on the table. "It's nice to see you all again."

The committee responded likewise. She pulled the sketches from inside the portfolio as she spoke. "I want to thank you all, especially you Tessa, for your polite rejection of what I had presented yesterday. It allowed me to respond with what I am about to present today." Setting up her laptop, she prepared it for the rotation of designs she had only on the computer. A rather old-fashioned chalk board hung on the wall, bordered at the bottom with a metal railing. The railing would perfectly hold the sketches she'd glued onto the same foam board to which the previous sketches had been mounted. Quickly, she lined them up, stepped back, started the laptop's slideshow, and began explaining her ideas.

Rory's black and white photography had been the final stimulus, the thing that had changed her improved concepts and made them perfect. To celebrate the small town, the window displays would *be* the small town. Portions of Connor Falls' easily recognized architecture would be reproduced in gray tones on oversized canvas, and still other buildings in somewhat smaller black and white rendering, adhered to wood panels cut to display them in shape and size. The only colors in the entire display would be the red Christmas balls stored in Hannah's basement, a touch of gold here and there, and potted evergreens decked in tiny white twinkle lights. And, of course, the store's merchandise would be highlighted.

Concluding her presentation, Nikki took a step away from her designs, her back to the committee members, and waited. No one said a word. Nikki's heart fluttered in her chest. A chair creaked.

Suddenly, the committee broke into applause.

"Bravo!" Tessa cried. "I can't believe you came up with all of that overnight!"

The other business owners expressed the same sentiment, using words like wonderful, perfect and we'll have to do something similar in our windows. Nikki crossed her arms over her chest, blinking back tears before she could turn and look at them.

"So, I guess you like it," she joked.

"Like it? I love it," Tessa enthused. "It's not only a celebration of Christmas but of Connor Falls itself."

"Maybe we should each purchase one of those canvas photos for our windows?" the bookstore owner suggested. "For cohesion throughout the town."

Someone seconded the proposal, followed by more agreement. Nikki drew in a deep, discreet breath.

"One thing," Gina said. "Nothing to be changed, because it's perfect, and really none of my business since these are Tessa's windows, but I'm wondering, can you really get this all prepared before Thanksgiving?"

Nikki had anticipated this question and had wondered about it herself. "Some of the items are in Hannah's storage. I would need to know where to purchase evergreens with wrapped root balls for later replanting—"

"Luke's," said Tessa. "Luke's Tree Farm. I can call him if you like, if you tell me how many you need."

Nikki thanked her. "As for the canvas, I have a supplier I contacted already and received an email in response before I headed out. If I get him the image files today, he has promised a three-day turnaround with expedited shipping. The only thing I might need help with, since I don't have the tools or the space, is cutting out the wood once I have the smaller photographs printed. I was going to check online for a local handyman, but perhaps someone here has a suggestion?"

"Rory," said Gina.

Nikki stilled inside, looking wordlessly at Gina.

"Did you meet him at the Jeffersons?"

"I did."

"He's great with this type of thing. He'd have the wood cut out in no time."

Nikki glanced around, hoping someone else would speak up, give another name. When they didn't, Nikka said, "He seems really busy right now with his work. I wouldn't want to bother him."

"I'm sure he wouldn't view it as a bother," Tessa chimed in.

"Get him out of his shell," said someone else.

"He needs to get involved in something besides work," said another.

And this, Nikki mused, was the problem with living in a small town. Everyone knew everybody else and had opinions about them. "I…okay. I'll ask him. But if you think of someone else, please text me or call. Leave me a message if I don't pick up. My cell phone number is on the business cards I handed out."

The meeting broke up after that. A dozen

business owners asked her for canvas prints as well before departing, in smaller sizes for their windows. Nikki took down their names and the images requested, said she would order them and deliver them with the bill. She stayed a few minutes after everyone had gone so she could speak with Tessa about a night to get everything set up when ready. With the night settled on, she left, too, determined to find a hardware store before the next morning so she could purchase a jigsaw and quite a few half sheets of thin wood panels to fit in her car. Maybe Sheila would let her work in the barn. There had been a local guy back in Brewster, a college kid, really, who had always helped her out with projects like these. Sometimes she'd work alongside him, but he usually didn't have the patience for it. Nikki would have to learn to fly solo with the cutting, and quickly.

Upon arrival at the Jeffersons, Nikki spotted Rory's truck in its usual spot. She avoided looking at it, or looking around for him, and went straight into the cottage. After lighting a fire, she placed the order for all the black and white prints. Per her conversation with Tessa, Nikki provided her supplier with the address for Hannah's since there would be too many canvases to transport in her car. After, huddled in a sweater against the chill, she proceeded to print out piecemeal drafts of the photos that would go on wood, cut them with scissors and taped them back into a whole. She would need them as templates to prepare the wood. She could manage that much, at least.

Simple, right? She supposed she would find out

soon enough.

Finishing the templates as the sun headed toward the horizon, Nikki laid them neatly on the bookcase. She took out a can of soup for dinner just as a knock sounded on the door.

"Coming!"

She opened the door to find Sheila standing outside and stepped back to let her in.

"Did you get my text about the rent?" Sheila asked as she entered.

"I'm sorry, yes, I did. I figured I would run over after I had my dinner."

Sheila waved a hand. "Oh, I wasn't rushing you! I just wanted to make sure you got it and the amount worked for you. And is that your dinner?" she added, nodding at the can on the small counter.

"Well, yes, soup it will be. It'll serve. And the rent is more than reasonable. Are you sure two hundred dollars a week is enough?"

"Quite enough, Nikki. Truly."

"Well, let me give you a check for this first week and a security deposit as well?"

"Just the two hundred."

Nikki smiled and grabbed her purse. "I was wondering," she began, opening it and digging around for her checkbook. "Might I stay through the end of the year? I know I should have asked that up front, but I find I have a liking for this town and, well, nowhere else to go. Feel free to say no, of course," she added with a self-conscious laugh, spinning around with the checkbook in hand.

"Nowhere else to go? For the holidays?" Sheila sounded appalled.

"I have no siblings. My parents are both gone. So, and less heartbreaking, is my apartment. The complex caught fire a few weeks ago. Everything I have left is in my car or in here."

"Goodness." Sheila sat down in the camp chair. "I never would have guessed."

"No reason you should have. I try not to advertise my loss."

"Of course, dear. I didn't mean that. So, you want to stay through the New Year?"

"If I could."

"You are quite welcome to do so. It'll be splendid. You'll need to get a Christmas tree in here, though. That is, if you celebrate?"

"I do."

"Wonderful. And Thanksgiving dinner? That's why I really came by. To see if you had any plans for Thanksgiving dinner. Pete and I would really like to have you. Not a huge gathering and as you were originally going to be here anyway?"

"Sounds wonderful," Nikki answered, even as she wondered if Rory might be part of the gathering. She wished she had worked out some way to find out before she blurted her agreement. Oh, well, they would have to make the best.

Sheila clapped her hands together beneath her chin like a gleeful child before hauling herself from the low-slung chair. Nikki wrote a hasty check for the six weeks and handed it to her. "Thank you so much, Sheila."

"Thank you, Nikki." Sheila headed for the door, pausing with her hand on the knob. "Oh, I nearly forgot. Pete…my husband Pete? He heard through the grapevine from the meeting today that you needed someone to help you with a few things for the window display."

"Yes, that's true. A little bit of woodwork. I'll pay him, naturally—"

"Oh, goodness, not Pete, although he'd be happy to, I'm sure. He thought Rory might give you a hand."

"Rory," Nikki said, recognizing the same tone she had used when Gina suggested him.

"Yes. The poor man needs to be part of something. Something other than work and grief. It's been nearly three years. Pete and I miss our daughter terribly, but Rory—"

"Rory's wife was your daughter? I didn't realize the connection. I put two and two together after a short conversation with Rory about the book of his I bought the other day, but I didn't realize he was your son-in-law. I'm sorry. I'm so sorry for your loss."

"Thank you, dear, so very much. And is, not was. We still consider Rory our son-in-law."

Nikki nodded. "Of course."

"He's just cleaning up now. I'll send him over to speak with you."

With that, she made her exit, leaving Nikki staring at the closed door. Nikki huffed out a short breath, confused and overwhelmed by the sudden emotions coursing through her. She decided to skip the soup until after Rory had been and gone and instead cut up an apple and cheese. The fruit and protein would stave off her hunger for a while and she could offer some to him, not necessarily as an icebreaker when he arrived, but as a distraction from whatever might be going through his head regarding Pete and Sheila's machinations. It might be prudent to tell him thanks but no thanks and muddle through herself, rather than let him be manipulated in this way.

Nikki barely heard the knock. For a big man, he managed a gentle, non-disruptive presence. She yanked open the door, looked up at him. She hadn't yet turned on the outside light and he stood in the door's thrown shadow. She couldn't see his face, couldn't read his expression, but she could tell by his stance he felt less than happy to be there.

"Come on in, Rory. Would you like a piece of apple? Cheese? I'm snacking before a can of soup a little later." She took the plate from the counter, held it out. He stood for an indecisive moment before coming in and closing the door, effectively cutting off the cold air that had been pouring in around him. The flames in the fireplace snapped back to attention, no longer shuddering in the breeze pushing through the space between the glass doors.

Rory reached out, grabbed a single apple slice from the plate and bit into it. "Thank you."

"Have as much as you like." She put the plate back on the counter. Rory went to the fire, held out his hands to the warmth. She remembered his hands. Remembered the way they held his cocktail, fingers dwarfing the glass, looking like they could just as easily crush it but holding the glass instead like he was used to protecting delicate things. Like flowers, maybe. Elusive images. His wife.

All those comparisons were only prompted by recent revelations. Back then, she hadn't understood, but she had been intrigued.

"So, I want to say again I'm sorry," Nikki announced from a negligible distance, given the room's size. "I've figured it out, timewise, but I certainly had no idea when we met."

"I know," he answered quietly. "That's the problem. You should have been able to tell, had I... It was like for an evening I forgot."

Nikki studied his back, his sloped shoulders, his bowed head. "But it was okay that you did. Without those moments or hours where the pain lets you go, grief is very difficult to survive."

He didn't turn from the fire. "Who did you lose?"

"My parents. It has been six for my mom and seven years for my dad now. I still miss them, though. I still get pain wafting into my consciousness now and again." Especially this time of year, she wanted to add, but she didn't.

He stared at the flames with his hands now shoved deep into his pockets. "Do you want help with…whatever it is?"

"Do you want to help? That's the more important question."

"Sure. Okay."

"I'll buy what I need tomorrow. Oh, do you have a jigsaw?"

He snorted, as near to a laugh as Nikki was going to get, she figured. Unlike that one evening. No wonder he felt guilty. She understood. She really did. But he needed to let it go. His wife surely would not want him grieving forever. Then again, who was Nikki to say? Each person released pain in their own way.

"Do I have a jigsaw?" he mimicked with a weak touch at humor. "You've seen my truck. I probably have one in the box in the bed right now."

Nikki smiled, trying to get him to relax. "Would you like me to show you what the job is?"

"Sure," he said again. Nikki pulled a few templates from the bookcase, held them out to him. He still hadn't fully looked at her.

"These are being printed and I just need a backer and something to stand each one up. I have about a dozen or so. Is that going to be a pain?"

He shook his head, lips compressed. "Did you take these?"

"I did," she said. "Yesterday. With my phone. I didn't have my camera with me."

His chest rose and fell. "They're very good."

"Thank you."

He studied them for another few minutes. She had no desire to interrupt him. He appeared to be thinking about something.

"Last night… no, this morning, actually, I was looking at the moon through the window and I…I wanted my camera again." He sounded surprised, shocked, bewildered, sad. But not happy. Not yet, Nikki figured. Maybe he would one day.

"It's a start," she said, easing the templates from his fingers.

"Yeah," he agreed, "it is."

He left with another apple slice and a piece of cheese in his grip. Nikki closed the door behind him. She peered around the curtain, watched him climb into his truck, back out from the spot by the barn and head onto the road. Nikki smoothed the fabric panel back in place, snatched up the soup can and peeled back the lid.

Rory Hollis was a broken soul. For sure, he was. But then, who wasn't? In some way or another, everyone had something broken in them. It was a matter of getting on with it, with life and goals and whatever the future might bring. Easier said than done, of course. Nikki understood that.

She also understood it wasn't her place to drag Rory Hollis back into the world. He had to do that himself.

Chapter Five

"What are you doing here at this hour?"

Rory gave his brother a long, level look. "You complain when you don't see me for weeks. Now you complain because I show up without, what, calling first?"

"I'm not complaining," Luke said, waving him inside. "I'm just surprised."

Hearing his voice, Rory's niece came screeching from her bedroom, dark hair flying. She thudded up against his legs.

"Uncle Rory!" Suddenly, she stepped back, eyeing him from beneath her bangs. "Are you okay?"

"It would take a lot more than that to hurt me," he said.

"I didn't mean—"

"I know what you meant, sweetie. And I'm fine."

Lydia had always been an intuitive child,

picking up on every little nuance among the adults around her. He remembered the day his wife passed. Everyone gathered in this house had wept. Except Lyddie. Tears in her eyes, but quiet and controlled, she had come and squirmed up onto the couch beside him, fitting her small hand into his, saying everything without a single word. She worried him sometimes, Lydia did. Yet, she was kid enough when the spirit took her. He would have liked one or two just like her, worries and all.

"Have you eaten yet?" Luke asked. "We're running a little behind tonight. I had to take the mini-x and dig up about a dozen of the smaller Frasers for the woman doing Hannah's windows. Tessa called me with the order. She said the two of you—you and the window person—met at your in-laws or something?"

"She's renting the old summer kitchen," Rory answered, leaving out any further details. "And sure, I'll eat. What's on?"

"Vegetarian chili. Don't ask," he added, jerking his head at his daughter with a crooked smile. "It's good. You'll like it. Lyddie, put another bowl out, will you?"

Lydia ran to do as asked and Rory followed her into the kitchen, lowering himself wearily into a chair at the table. He pushed his hands through his hair. "Where's—"

"Working," Lyddie answered before Luke could. Smiling, she skipped from the room. "Be right back," she called over her shoulder.

Luke glanced at him from the stove. Rory bit his lip, waiting.

"So," Luke said, "you got booted back home. How's that going?"

"To be honest, better than expected. To be more honest, still not good."

Luke nodded in commiseration, but said nothing. There was nothing to be said. Rory wasn't quite sure Luke understood exactly what he continued to deal with, yet that was all right. Luke would be there for him, always had been despite the years between him and his younger brother.

Luke popped open the oven and reached in with an oven mitt, pulling out a tray of browned rolls.

"Yours?" Rory asked doubtfully.

"Who are you kidding? Gina's." Luke dumped the tray into a waiting wooden basket. "Just heated them up a bit."

Lydia appeared with a fluffy seen-better-days stuffed rabbit and hopped into the seat next to Rory's. Luke settled the chili pot onto a heat-proof mat and shoved a ladle down inside. "Informal tonight."

"Every night," Lyddie chimed in.

"Every night," Luke agreed and ladled chili into the three bowls, grabbed the butter from the fridge in case someone wanted it for a roll, and sat down. He scooted his chair closer to the table. After a second, he shoved a container filled with some sort of shaved cheese in Rory's direction. "For on top. Perfect."

"So, it's not wholly vegetarian," Rory commented.

Luke arched his dark brows. "One can choose

to imbibe or not." Across from her father, Lydia giggled.

Rory's lips turned up. It felt good to be in his brother's house. As he ate, they discussed the upcoming holidays, including Thanksgiving, and skirted around any invitations. For now. Rory expected to receive one for something at some point. In the living room, a space had already been cleared for the tree which would soon grace the area. Above and to the right of the fireplace Rory's own work hung framed, numerous black and white images he had taken depicting Luke and his small family in ways as artistic as they were personal. Rory hadn't been able to help himself. Catching intimacy as well as light and shadow and composition was what he did best. He viewed it as a gift, this skill. He certainly hadn't gone out of his way to learn it. He had always been grateful to have been given that talent, though. Until...

Well, it was starting to come back to him, the longing to capture beauty and honesty and special, quiet moments. The yearning for that distinct light of winter, too. Something about gray wintry skies, from late Autumn on through the coldest months, always drew him in.

"Winter light," Luke said softly, following Rory's gaze to a point above the mantel where a photo of Luke and Lydia at the iced-over pond hung.

"Winter light," said Rory.

"Had any of your cameras out recently?"

Rory shook his head. Again, Luke said nothing, but this time he wanted to. Rory could see it in his eyes, in the muscle twitching momentarily in his jaw.

"I'm getting there," Rory said.

Luke smiled at him. "I know you are. Now dig in. Lyddie cut up all the veggies, added the spices, opened cans. Dumped everything in the pot. Stirred it. Taste-tested it."

"In other words, she made it."

"Uh-huh, and it's delicious, so eat." Luke winked broadly at his daughter.

Rory did, surprising himself by finishing the bowl and going for seconds. He lifted his hand to meet Lydia's in a high-five. "Good job, Lyddie."

"Thanks, Uncle Rory."

"So," Luke asked around a mouthful, "what's this window…person like? What does she call herself anyway? Window designer? That doesn't sound right."

"A window display designer? Window dresser? I don't know. I didn't actually ask." But he had. That long ago evening. She'd told him she designed window displays, which would probably make window display designer the most accurate title.

"What's her name?"

"Nikki."

Some clue to his unrest must have crept out with her name, because both his brother and his niece looked more intently at him. Rory concentrated on the chili, avoiding their gazes.

"Nice enough?"

"Yep," said Rory, biting into a buttered roll and taking his time to chew the mouthful, his eyes on the spoon in his other hand.

Luke rubbed his face, watched Rory through his fingers, finally turned to Lydia. "Lyddie, are you finished eating?"

"Yeah, Dad," she said. "I'll go to my room and do something there so you and Uncle Rory can talk."

Beside her, Rory snorted, shook his head. Luke's mouth curved.

"She's pretty amazing," said Luke, once she had closed the door to her room. "Scares me sometimes."

"I'm not surprised," Rory answered. Whether about the amazing part or the scary reference, Luke didn't ask and Rory didn't say, although he had meant both. He finished his remaining food in silence. Normally, Luke got up right away to clear the table, but tonight he sat on, toying with the crumbs on the bread plate by his empty bowl.

Rory blew out a breath through his nose. "What?"

"I'm just asking about your life. Looks like I upset you. Was this woman rude to you?"

Standing, Rory lifted his bowl and Lydia's from the table, carried them to the counter and set them beside the sink. "She wasn't rude. She's far from rude. She's funny and sweet, in fact," he added, surprised he could manage to admit it.

Luke appeared beside him with more dishes and began rinsing them before placing each item in the dishwasher. "All that in the course of how many minutes?"

"Five hours," Rory said.

"Five hours?"

"Yes. Five hours only months after I lost Kat. At that thing I had in Manhattan. We talked. A lot." Rory bit down on the flesh inside his cheek, trying hard not to remember.

"That's a bit of a coincidence, then," said Luke, sounding uncertain the possibility such coincidence existed. Rory nipped that in the bud.

"She didn't even remember me. Not when we were first introduced. She did later, but not in those few minutes. I guess I've changed since the party. I hadn't even wanted to go."

Luke closed the dishwasher door. "You have changed, Rory," he said. "We've all seen it, felt it. Heck, you dropped a lot of weight since then, too. And your hair, well…we won't go on about your hair."

"Shut up," Rory chided, smiling despite himself.

"So, a woman you got on well with a couple years ago has made an incredibly coincidental reappearance in your life. What's the problem? Because it is a problem. You can't hide that face from me, brother."

Rory filled his lungs, let the air out. Slowly. "The problem is, we got on well a couple years ago. That never should have happened."

"I—" Whatever his brother had been about to say was cut short by Lydia's exit from her bedroom dressed in her pajamas, a hairbrush in her hand. She walked straight up to her dad. Wordlessly, he took the brush and began to run it through Lyddie's long, dark hair.

"The things I do for love," he muttered with a

good-natured smile.

Yes, thought Rory, wincing in memory, the things one did for love couldn't easily be cast aside.

Or forgotten.

*   *   *

Despite her nearly sleepless night previously, Nikki stayed awake much later than planned looking again through Rory's photography book. Fascinating, beautiful, evocative, the images still made her wonder why she chose to torture herself with sympathy for a man she barely knew.

"Enough," she finally said out loud. She closed the book and slipped it carefully onto the floor beside the low bed. Reaching up, she switched off the lamp on the wall above the metal headboard. Darkness washed the room for the space of a second and then her eyes adjusted, revealing the upstairs area bathed in a silvery luminescence. Something delicate brushed the glass. Flinging back the covers, Nikki hurried to the window.

A light snow fell through the moonlight and had already coated bare branches in pale pencil strokes, dusted the barn. In the yard below the snow clung to seedheads and grasses, all highlighted by the moon's white glow. Although not yet winter, it seemed a perfect image of seasonal tranquility and beauty. Rather than run down the stairs for her camera, she grabbed the phone and threw open the window, leaning out and taking multiple photos. If one turned out good enough, she'd make it her Christmas card this year. Peace on Earth.

Her own existence had been anything but

tranquil lately, yet staring out at the snowy scene a certain peace traced its way through her body, seeping into bones and muscle and the convoluted gray matter of her brain. She shut the window and closed her eyes, willing the stress to go, at least for the next few weeks. She decided quite deliberately to pretend everything had been riddled and solved and she had moved on to a place where complications did not exist.

Hugging herself against the chill she had let into the room, she thought about Rory, about his dark, shuttered gaze, the constant shadow on his jaw and in his expression. She thought about him laughing that long ago evening and wondered again if he laughed at all anymore.

Returning to her bed, Nikki climbed beneath the covers, tugging them up to her chin and shivering. She stared up at the patterns dancing across the ceiling and thought about a man she hadn't recognized, yet once remembered couldn't get out of her mind.

Tomorrow he would be helping her. Reluctantly, she knew. However, she wouldn't argue or pretend she didn't need his assistance. She could likely manage to cut the wood herself, but not in a timely fashion, and she only had a matter of days to get everything together for Hannah's windows.

In the morning, somewhat later in the morning than she would have liked, she woke and showered and stuffed in some toast and tea before heading out to her car. Rory's truck sat in its usual spot, but he'd already unloaded and gone inside. Sheila's SUV was there, too. Pete had gone for the day, to the hardware store they owned. Nikki planned to stop there for the wood, if they had it. It would be wrong to shop elsewhere. The place with the hometown feel had managed to instill certain inclinations in only three days.

Jefferson's Hardware held a strong position outside the town on a main road. Still, it maintained its quaint façade and appeal. Nikki pulled into a vacant spot and went inside. She found Pete Jefferson at the register himself. She recognized him from a photo on the Jefferson's kitchen mantelpiece. He looked up from the coffee cup held to his lips. Like Sheila, he appeared to be in his late fifties or so, but he possessed a shock of thick, bone-white hair. He wore it on the long side, curling over his shirt collar. Something about that defiant flag made Nikki like him instantly.

She held out her hand. "Hi. I'm Nikki. Your renter. And you're Pete. It's nice to finally meet you."

He took her fingers in his large hand and shook them. "Nice to meet you finally, too. What brings you in here? Nothing wrong with the plumbing at the cottage or anything, I hope?" His eyes twinkled at his teasing.

"Nope, all's good there. I've come for some wood, like luan sheets, only a little thicker?"

"Right, for Tessa's window displays."

Yes, the homeliness of small towns was already luring her in, but the way everyone seemed to know everybody else had not yet endeared her. She had been used to a little more anonymity. Not that she was surprised he knew about her need. He'd been the one to recommend Rory to help her, after all.

"I'd need the sheets cut down to four feet, if that's possible. I won't fit them in my car otherwise."

"We have half sheets. I'll get Jeremy to give you a hand." He came out from behind the counter to accompany Nikki while calling to a tall young man with auburn hair. Jeremy ambled over as they approached.

"Nikki, Jeremy. Jeremy, Nikki needs—how many?"

"Better make if fourteen," Nikki said, "to be on the safe side in case one of them cracks or is otherwise damaged."

Pete gave a nod. "You can bring back what you don't use."

"Thanks."

"And with Rory helping, you shouldn't have any ending up unreturnable due to mishap."

Nikki arched a brow. "Meaning, if it's me doing it, there might be? I'm not denying the possibility, but I could be insulted by the implication."

Jeremy laughed, a quick, stifled guffaw, and exchanged a look with his employer.

"I didn't mean that," Pete said.

"I know you didn't. I was joking. Sorry. You don't know me well enough to pick up on my attempt at humor, I guess."

Pete shot her a sidelong glance. "I only meant that Rory is an excellent carpenter. He's wasted on the painting he's doing for us right now, but he insists on doing it all."

"He's an excellent photographer, too," Nikki said. "A shame he's given it up."

"So, you know about that, do you?"

Nikki nodded.

"Yes, well, Sheila and I pray regularly he'll come back to us, if not the way he was, at least a happy man again."

"I'm sorry for your loss, too, Pete," Nikki said quietly.

Pete stilled for a moment, his gaze on something Nikki couldn't see, reminding her that as parents they continued to grieve in their own way, too. "Fourteen, then," he said with a sudden, brisk nod. "I'll ring you up and Jeremy will load them in your car. Anything else you need?"

"Sandpaper, wood glue, a pint of black, satin enamel and a brush," Nikki rattled off without taking the time to pull out her list. She regretted the pain she'd brought to Pete Jefferson's eyes. Not raw and new, but there, like a dull ache. Sheila hid, or coped with it, better than her husband.

Pete engaged in several side trips on their way back to the counter, piling everything into a cardboard box for her once he'd scanned the prices into the register. Nikki paid him for everything with an apology for having reminded him of his pain.

"No need to apologize. Your sentiments are appreciated."

Nikki left and met Jeremy by her car, reflecting on the fact losing a philandering boyfriend and an apartment full of possessions was by no means the end of the world.

Chapter Six

With the wood loaded in her trunk and back seat, Nikki pulled up into the space now designated as hers at the Jefferson's. She had stopped at Hannah's to physically view the items stored in the basement. She also made final interior measurements of the windows, and purchased a down comforter and some boot-like slippers so she wouldn't be trudging around in her pjs and her regular boots at night. The floors were quite chilly in the cottage, even with the area rug centered on the floor planks.

Nikki carried the bagged goods in first, then stood in indecision behind her open trunk, trying to decide where she should put the wood. She had no idea where she and Rory would be working. It didn't seem likely they'd be using a jigsaw inside the cottage. She could just imagine the sawdust spraying everywhere. She stepped back, reached for the trunk lid to shut it. Better to leave everything in the car than move it twice.

"I've got that."

Nikki spun to find Rory striding rather silently across the yard. "I didn't know where to put them."

"Pete and Sheila are letting us use the barn. I can set the wood in there and free up your car. We'll cut it later this evening."

Nikki wasn't about to let him carry it all. She reached into the trunk, grabbed several panels, handed them to him. He took the pile with a startled expression. Lifting out the remainder, she followed him.

"I wasn't playing the tough male card, there," he said. "I promise."

"I know," said Nikki, but she hadn't been so sure.

She'd always been willing to pull her weight, only paying someone to do those things she hadn't the knowledge for or which she physically could not manage. She dove right into any project, even with Ted, sometimes only stopping when she hit a block she really ought to have recognized in the beginning. She often wondered if this had been the underlying source for Ted's dissatisfaction with their relationship. He wanted to be the caretaker, the provider, for her to require him in that capacity, in any capacity. To *need* him, not only want him in her life. That wasn't her. Hadn't been. Never would be.

When the last of the wood had been stacked neatly on a work table, Nikki took a moment to look around at the various tools and stations for woodworking. "Sweet setup," she said.

Rory's brows lowered. "Do you do any

woodworking? I thought—"

"I love the idea of it," she interrupted. "So far, though, I'm not that much good at actually doing it. I cut myself quite a few years back." She raised her left arm, shoved back her jacket and sweater sleeve, exposing a long scar. "Since then, I've avoided trying to learn on my own. Hence, yes, needing help with a jigsaw."

"But you'd like to learn."

"I'm a little afraid since the accident, even though it's been a long time. I want to get over that."

"And what would you do with your knowledge?" Rory seemed genuinely interested although slightly amused. Like he might be trying to wrap his head around some strange construction she wanted to make. Hopefully he visualized purpose, too, because she wasn't inclined to be frivolous.

"I'd make things. Picture frames. Benches. A really cool desk. Maybe some extraordinary outdoor Christmas décor."

"So, simple things," he said with a chuckle.

Nikki smiled. "What would you consider simple?"

He reflected a moment, his brown eyes searching the air in thought. "A cutting board."

"A cutting board?"

"You'd get the feel for the machinery, for the wood. You could rout the edges if you wanted to try that, then sand the piece, finish it accordingly. Many of the things you'd do for a more complicated piece. You know, work up to the really cool desk."

Nikki's lips twisted, fighting back a laugh. "But…a cutting board. Really?"

"Why not? They always come in handy. We could start with that."

She saw the 'we' hit him the same instant it did her. For her, the slip was merely curious and confusing. For him, it appeared to be devastation.

He turned hastily away. "I have to get back to work. Would you mind shutting the door when you leave?"

He had disappeared into the cold November air before she could get another word out. Nikki followed a moment later, pulling the door closed behind her. A haunted man was Rory Hollis. It hurt her heart to recognize just how much.

*   *   *

Nikki spent the afternoon hours diagraming the precise layout for each window. She would need the visual if she hoped to get the displays set up in record time. She'd gotten an idea what merchandise Tessa intended to put into each window and planned accordingly. Finally satisfied, she looked up from her work and realized the sun had descended, just visible beyond the nearest hill.

She rose and stretched and went to answer the soft knock. Upon opening the door, she found Rory on the other side looking torn between leaving and staying. She figured his promise to help her was the only thing keeping him from giving in to the former. She stepped back as he entered, his dark head inches from the nearest beam.

"Would you like some soup?" she asked him. "I haven't gotten back to the grocery store yet, but I do have another can. Chicken noodle, I think."

He hesitated. "I'm good, but you go ahead."

"I can't do that."

He jerked around, looking her in the eye. "Why not?"

"Because it would be impolite. Not only that, but what would you do while I ate it?"

He jerked a thumb over his shoulder. "I could get a start on—"

"No. The soup'll take five minutes to make and even less time to eat. I'm sharing the can with you, Rory, all right? It's not like it's a date or anything."

She wasn't quite sure why she'd uttered the last, but it seemed that statement and the annoyance in her tone convinced him her offer held no hidden agenda. He released a quiet breath and nodded before going to settle himself on the hearth edge, his long legs drawn up and bent sharply at the knees. He rested his arms across them.

"You could use another chair," he said.

She pivoted away from him to start preparing their meal, such as it were. "Maybe I'll make one."

She'd meant her words as a joke, to perhaps ease the tension from his earlier reaction in the barn, but clearly, he hadn't taken them that way.

He sat in silence behind her. Dumping the soup in a pan, she spun back around to face him. "Look, I—"

Her heart plummeted into her stomach. She didn't believe he even remembered she stood nearby. Glued to the floor between his feet, his gaze reflected something she never wanted to feel.

"Rory?"

His head came up slowly, dragged away from memory.

"Are you okay?"

"Yeah," he said.

Doubtful, Nikki thought in response, but didn't say it. Instead, she went back to the stove, turned on the burner, grabbed two bowls from the cabinet next to it. "Five minutes. Just give me five minutes."

"Take your time." He sounded somewhat recovered from wherever he had gone.

Nevertheless, *run,* Nikki's voice whispered in her head. Run away from this situation, from this suffering man. She took a deep breath, let it out through her nose, picked up a spoon and vigorously stirred the soup in its pot, deciding with determination she would not run. He needed a friend. A friend who hadn't been part of the whole life he'd lived with his wife. No matter how uncomfortable he felt around Nikki, she could still be that. For the next several weeks, she absolutely could.

Pouring the steaming soup into each bowl,

she placed them on plates surrounded by crackers and carried Rory's to him at the hearth. Retrieving hers, she lowered herself into the camp chair.

"Thanks," he said.

"No problem."

They ate in silence, a silence more comfortable than awkward, at least. At the conclusion, she gathered everything back up and placed it all in the sink, running water into each piece to keep until she returned later. She heard Rory get up from the hearth, groaning a little. In stiffness, she supposed. He couldn't possibly have been comfortable seated there. As he made his way to the door, his footsteps vibrated the floorboards.

"Thanks, Nikki. I'll meet you over there." When the door closed behind him, she realized it was the first time he'd spoken her name in the past few days without sounding as though he might choke on it.

Prepared for the barn's chill in her heavy coat, Nikki gathered up the templates and followed him over a few minutes later. She walked into blessed warmth. He'd already started up a space heater on the wall not far from the work area and had cleared two benches, laying out as many boards as would fit in the space.

"Templates?" he asked, holding out his hand. Nikki handed them over.

"I got painters tape to hold them down. I figured that would work."

"It will, indeed," he said. In no time, multiple boards were ready for cutting. Rather than a jigsaw, Rory used Pete's bandsaw to cut the pieces. Nikki handed him each panel and watched through the safety glasses he handed her. She removed the template afterward and set the wood aside for sanding and painting.

"Your turn?" he asked when she handed him the next to the last templated piece.

Nikki stepped up to the machine. "I'll give it a try."

Rory provided careful but not annoyingly precise instruction. With his guidance, she cut the two templates on the four-by-four-foot panel out, and had forgotten her fear of sharp, toothed blades.

"You want the last one, too?"

"Sure," she said, positioning the wood as he had done and cutting the intricate design without a single word from him. Once she'd switched the bandsaw off and pulled the plug from the outlet the way she'd been taught way back when, before the mishap, she swept the machine clean, depositing the sawdust in a nearby bin. She turned to find Rory studying her.

"What?"

He shook his head. "You've been around a woodshop before."

"Well, yeah," she drawled. "I was mostly teaching myself with the dubious tutelage of a kid back when I was in high school. And then this happened." She pointed at the place where the old scar marked her arm, hidden beneath her coat. "After that I would help, but wouldn't do."

"You seemed rather fearless just now."

"That probably had something to do with the person doing the teaching."

"I wasn't teaching," he said.

Nikki removed her safety glasses, set them down. "You were, whether you realized it or not. Every step of the way, I saw you checking to make sure I was paying attention. And whenever you spoke, to explain something you were doing, or when I took over, you were clear but not full of terms I might not know. It helps, having that guidance. Certain, and not like you expect me to fail."

"Is that what happened with this kid, this high school friend?"

"Oh, yeah. I think he was setting me up all along for an epic fail. I wish I had a picture of his face when the blood started spurting. I don't think an accident had been his actual intent."

Rory looked momentarily horrified before he burst into a laugh. "Do you speak to him, this kid now man?"

"I ran into him at a reunion a few years back. He avoided me as if I had some contagious disease. Can you imagine carrying guilt like that around for so long?"

Nikki knew she had said the wrong thing as soon as Rory turned away. She wanted to apologize, but she had no reason to. She had related a story and her feelings about it. Whatever reaction he had to it was his and his alone. She'd directed nothing cruel or unfeeling at him. He would have to get past it on his own. Any apology from her would only make it easier for him to hold on to his pain rather than allow it to heal. Whatever time he needed, he needed, sure. She understood that need. However, she refused to tiptoe around him.

"If you have to get on and it's okay for me to stay in here, I'll sand and paint these," she said, reaching for the sandpaper.

"I've nowhere I have to be just yet," Rory said, turning back to her. "Want to give the belt sander a try? It'll be a lot quicker than doing them by hand, although you'll still have to do the tricky bits with paper."

She nodded agreement and walked over to the machine, where he began briefly explaining the operation. She watched his hands, noticing how large and strong and sure they appeared. Scarred a bit, too. Not pampered hands by any means. Beautiful hands, though.

It took Nikki a moment to realize he'd stopped speaking. She jerked her head up, back to his face, realizing she likely possessed a deer-in-the-headlights expression.

His brows came down. "Are you okay?"

"Yep," she said.

"Ready to start?"

She nodded, stepping up to the sander, where he positioned a cut board. He handed her the safety glasses. She put them on. "Got it," she said.

"Safety first."

He helped her adjust the cut-out for the photo of the church in town, his fingers brushing hers. He didn't jerk away as she expected him to, but did slowly pull his hand from contact and shove it down deep into his pocket. Yet he stayed on beside her, encouraging her technique and even laughing once or twice. Nothing reminded her more of the man she had briefly known than his laughter. For his own sake, she wished he enjoyed more of it.

When Nikki had sanded the last, operating for some time alone, she noticed Rory had cleaned up the scraps from cutting and had been applying sand paper to the tight areas on all the wood backers while she worked. She glanced at her watch, shocked to find the time after nine o'clock.

"I'm sorry! It's really getting late. I didn't mean to keep you so long. Would you mind helping me carry these into the cottage? I can spread the tarp I picked up and paint them in there, then leave them overnight to dry."

Wordlessly, he obliged, piling them all against the wall inside the main living area. After, he stood next to Nikki, studying them.

"They look good," he said.

"Don't they? I mean…well, yes, don't they? Thank you so much. Let me get my wallet. I never asked how much you wanted for—"

"Nothing."

"But I—"

"I don't want anything, Nikki. I don't want you to pay me. I...I kind of needed that. I don't want money for it."

He left then, without a goodbye, shutting the door quietly behind him.

Chapter Seven

For a full five minutes, Rory sat behind the wheel staring through the truck window at the barn where he had spent more than three hours working with Nikki. The perpetual knot in his stomach had eased about half an hour in. Partway through the evening, he had discovered himself content to be there. The feeling baffled him. After all this time, he didn't quite know what to make of it.

Yet with recognition the same old guilt and remembered loss came rushing in. Well, maybe not quite the same. He still experienced the familiar ache and dissatisfaction with himself, but it felt...different. He didn't know if he liked the difference. Change was always good. He had said that enough times himself. But this change, this tiny little change, still fluttered in his heart like a betrayal.

He'd have to get past it, because he planned to help Nikki again. Everything needed to be transported, set up. He used to thoroughly enjoy Christmas, thrown himself into it with Kat, sharing her joy and exuberance. He'd spent the past few holed away as much as possible during the holiday. Helping to set up those windows could be a step back into the season's light. He needed that. He needed *something*.

Glancing in the sideview mirror before backing up, he caught movement. In boots not fully zippered, Sheila hurried clumsily across the driveway in his direction. Putting the truck into park once more, Rory climbed out.

Sheila stopped breathlessly a few feet away. "Rory, I'm glad I caught up with you."

"What's up?"

"I'm not taking no for an answer this year, Rory."

His stomach sank a little.

"Seriously," she went on, "I want you here for Thanksgiving dinner. There won't be a lot of people. You can be as surly as you like. I just want you to be there with us. It's been too long."

Rory stared at her. He drew a breath in, let it out long and slow, frosting the frigid night air. Then he did something neither expected. Not him, and surely not Sheila. He stepped forward and hugged his former mother-in-law, coat-covered shoulders wrapped in his arms.

"Okay," he said into her hat-covered hair, and released her, stepping back. "Okay. I give in. What time?"

She gazed up at him, her eyes suspiciously moist. "Three o'clock. Or any time before that. You know I'm not one to turn down help."

"Okay," he said again, watching her turn and make her way back to the house, probably too stunned for further words. After she shut the door with another look in his direction, he got back in his truck and headed home.

Home. He hadn't thought of the house as home since the day Kat died. But it had been. More than home. His wife, the house they shared, the town, their endeavors and hopes, his life. He'd put his heart into the book Nikki had brought to him the day she realized his identity. A book titled *Home* for a reason.

He inserted his key into the door handle, unlocked it, pushed the door open, stepped inside, one booted foot following the other. His rubber soles made soft vibrations on the floor. Echoed into a strange emptiness. The house smelled empty, too, as if nothing took place there. No lingering coffee smell, no food or perfume or lately watered plants. Kat would have hated the house as it had become. He knew she would.

Especially in the coming months. This close to Thanksgiving, she would already have begun decorating. Soon, the house would be filled with the scent of cinnamon and cranberry and spruce. Baked goods. Special meals. The sound of laughter and music filling the air most nights and many days. She'd loved voices raised in song, had been a choir member up until nearly the end. Kat loved company. Loved family.

Rory had turned his back on all of it.

He'd turned away from his own pursuits as

well. Kat would have hated that more than anything else. Shirking his coat off, Rory swung it up onto the coat rack, the cold, sweet air from the garment drifting around his chilled face. Something else, too. A light scent, somewhat spicy. Not Sheila. Nikki. Her coat had been hanging over his in the barn.

Chewing on his inner lip, he strode quickly across the house and up the stairs to shower, glancing into the bedroom where he hadn't slept since…the last time. The moonlight fell across the barren mattress like snow. Stopping dead, he retraced his steps back to the doorway and gazed inside. After a moment he went in, circled around to the dresser, pulled open empty drawers. He shut them noiselessly and lowered himself onto the mattress edge.

So, this was his life. Unless he decided to change it.

* * *

Nikki rose early Sunday morning to finish preparing the wood cutouts. Canvases and photos had been scheduled for delivery on Tuesday. Therefore, despite the imminent deadline, Nikki found herself with some surprising free time. First, she popped into ask Sheila what she might want her to bring to Thanksgiving dinner.

Sheila promptly replied, "Surprise me."

"You may be sorry," Nikki joked.

"I doubt it, dear."

Suddenly, Nikki heard Rory's voice in a back room. It appeared he might be talking to someone on his phone.

"His brother," said Sheila, although Nikki hadn't asked. No doubt, the woman had caught the shift in Nikki's attention. Self-conscious, Nikki excused herself and left, walking swiftly and with manufactured intent toward her car.

The clear night had given way to a cloudy day. With no plans before the afternoon but a trip to the grocery store to stock up and buy ingredients to bake something for Thanksgiving, Nikki took the time to drive up and down hilly local roads rather than make straight for the market. Farm land gave way to small communities and back to fields, then woods, and little cul-de-sacs of homes once more. Quaint, short bridges spanned tumbling creeks. Numerous fieldstone houses, some with date stones aging them to the colonial era, still sat firmly ensconced on vast acreage. Yes, little by little, Nikki was falling in love with Connor Falls and the surrounding environs.

She could have stayed in the temporary residence she'd acquired in Brewster while the apartment complex was being rebuilt. Although she'd finished the winter window designs for local businesses in the summer months, she'd received other job offers that would have kept her busy through the season. But her ties to the area had broken. When she received the call from Tessa, having been referred in a very convoluted manner, she'd been anxious to take the job no matter how crazy it seemed to commit to the endeavor at such a late date.

It all seemed a bit like fate. She didn't believe

in fate, though. Coincidence, sure, and definitely one's choices. But not fate.

Spotting a sign for Luke's Tree Farm and remembering it from discussion at the meeting, Nikki turned onto the side road and up the lane leading to the establishment. Evergreens in multiples varieties covered the hillside beyond the huge red barn and the quite adorable house not far from it. It appeared a few people were keen on getting their trees home and ready by Thanksgiving Day, but the graveled lot was far from full. No doubt it would be as soon as the season hit.

Nikki parked her car a little away from the others and got out. A man with short-cropped, sandy hair stepped out from the barn. Nikki headed over to him. He turned at her footsteps.

"Hi," he said. "I'm Frank. Can I help you?"

So, maybe Luke's wasn't owned by an actual Luke. Nikki nodded at the man. "I'm Nikki. Hi. Do I have to cut my own, or do you or someone else cut them down? Not that I want it today. I thought I might look at the trees, see what sizes and kinds you have. Do you tag them for customers? I would take a live one, but I have no place to put it after."

She realized she was rambling, but she couldn't help it. She'd just caught sight of a man who resembled Rory so closely she thought he must be Rory's brother. Coincidence was mounting at an extraordinary rate.

Frank pivoted in the man's direction, lifted a hand. "Luke! This customer would like to tag a tree. I'll grab a tag and take her up?"

"I've got it," said Luke. "There's a couple

coming down with two cut trees. They'll need to be wrapped."

"Sure thing, boss," Frank answered and left them to meet the couple in question.

Luke glanced down at her boots and nodded in approval. "Come on, I'll write your name on a tag and we'll head into the fields. Do you know what type you want?"

"A balsam or a Fraser, if you have them?" said Nikki, following him into the barn. "Not too big. The place I'm staying doesn't have a lot of room."

Luke opened a drawer in a work bench and pulled out a bright orange, wired, wooden tag along with a waterproof marker. "Name?"

"Sharp. Nikki."

His hand checked a moment above the tag before he wrote out her name in a quick, easy script. "You're the window dresser," he said while the pen moved.

Nikki's mouth twisted at his tone. "I am the window dresser, yes."

"I have some trees balled in burlap for Hannah's that Tessa bought. Reduced price, because I'm taking them back after. She gave me your number to call about the delivery time. I was going to do that later today." Straightening, he looked her in the eye. "You're staying at the cottage at the Jefferson place, aren't you?"

"Yes. Is Rory put out by my presence?" She hadn't meant to ask it, hadn't meant to bring up his brother at all. It seemed like talking behind somebody's back. And yet, she really wanted to know to what extent her being there bothered him.

Luke chuckled. "Ah, a bit. He'll get over it."

Not likely, Nikki thought. He appeared pretty entrenched in a place where any change could rattle him. "I hope so," she said. "I didn't mean to inconvenience anyone."

Luke made a dismissive noise, although she spotted the concern in the eyes so much like Rory's. "He'll come around. Ready? Let's go find you a tree."

They spent the next twenty-five minutes walking among the fragrant evergreens, Luke asking friendly questions, answering some of hers, even talking briefly about his brother. He pointed out a pond far below them, explaining a photo Luke had hanging on his wall.

"Your brother's an amazing photographer," Nikki said. "I bought his book in town before I realized who he was. I…we met before."

"He told me."

"Did he? Anyway, it's such a weird happenstance, running into him again. I had no idea about his wife. I think I've stuck my foot in it a couple of times since showing up."

"He'll be okay. He has to be. I want my brother back."

The raw admission pierced Nikki's heart. Luke hadn't issued it in disturbance or grief, however. More a statement of fact.

"I have Douglass fir over here," he said, jerking his chin, back to business. "They've got this citrusy smell that's really nice. I have some small, recent plantings, too, so I could dig one up for you. I heard what you said to Frank. I know you have no place to plant it after, but you could donate the tree to the park in the center of town."

"That's a great idea," Nikki said with a smile. "Show me."

With a three-foot tree tagged in her name, Nikki and Luke returned to the parking lot. On the way, he showed her the assorted evergreens he'd dug up with a machine for the windows. "Tessa gave me sizes. These all right?"

Nikki nodded. "Perfect. Now I just need tubs. In the right color," she added, rolling her eyes.

"I've got a bunch of square, wooden crates in the loft. You'll have to paint them. You can come back later with the paint if you want to do that. I'll have Rory pick them up in his truck tomorrow and deliver them to the store. You can meet him there, get them put wherever Tessa wants them until you're ready to get them in the windows."

"I don't want to put anyone out," Nikki said reflexively.

"You're not. Believe me. This may be just what my brother needs. He used to love the holidays. I'm going to get him back to that place if I have to drag him kicking and screaming."

Nikki had a sudden mental picture involving Rory's lumberjack frame in Santa attire being dragged by the ankles through the evergreens by his somewhat—although not by much—smaller brother. She fought against laughter.

Luke grinned. "What? You're picturing that, aren't you?"

"Well, yeah," she said. "In ridiculous detail."

Luke laughed, then sobered. "Don't let him get

you down, Nikki. His heartbreak is tangible and contagious if you let it. None of us do. We all miss Kat. Everyone misses her. But she was an unselfish and happy individual in life and I feel quite sure she would in no way want him to grieve forever."

"Understood." Nikki reached for her car door handle. "What time should I come back?"

"Around seven? I'll have the lights on in there."

Nikki thanked Luke and climbed into her vehicle, watching him stroll back to the barn. Shoulders relaxed, head level. Rory had held himself in that way when she'd met him. It would be nice to see him do so again. Not that it was any business of hers. Or her worry. Or her duty. But it would be nice.

… Chapter Eight

True to his word, Luke Hollis had turned on the lights in his barn and was waiting for her when she showed up. Nikki hefted the gallon of steel gray paint from her trunk, together with a brush, leaving the bags containing Christmas lights, picture wire and hooks inside. Prancing a little at his side and bundled up in a pink coat and matching boots, a dark-haired girl smiled at Nikki as she approached. Luke introduced the child as Lydia, his daughter.

"Pleased to meet you," said Nikki, tucking the brush beneath her arm in order to shake the little girl's extended hand.

"I've got everything set up for you," said Luke. "Upstairs. I pulled the best crates out already so you wouldn't have to dig for them. When you're finished, just shut off the light switch down here and slip the lock onto the door." He indicated a padlock hanging from the open latch. "And if the door gives you any trouble, come up to the house and get me."

Thanking him again for his kindness to someone he didn't know at all, Nikki went into the large structure and stood a moment breathing in the scents, the most prevalent being from the evergreen cuttings stacked against the wall beside several boxes filled with wreath rings. She supposed Luke and his employees would be tackling wreath-making next. She would make sure to stop back to purchase one.

In the loft, she located the work area. Luke had, indeed, piled more than a dozen crates into neat piles. Newspaper lay folded on the workbench for her use. She spread it out, popped open the can with an opener she had purchased along with the paint, centered the first crate on the paper. Spotting a radio nearby, she turned it on for background noise and set to work. She had a lot to get through and didn't want to keep Luke up late, worrying about whether or not she'd gone and left the barn door open or anything.

Singing along to early Christmas music being played by a local radio station, Nikki had lifted the fifth crate onto the bench for painting when she heard a noise in the barn below. She flicked down the radio volume.

"Hello?"

A step thudded on the narrow staircase. Nikki dropped the brush onto the newspaper and grabbed a nearby broom, hurrying over to the stairs and peering down into the dim illumination below, spying a tall body, dark head bent and looking at the underside of his boot. "Luke?" Nikki called. The head jerked, Rory's now familiar face looking up at her.

"Sorry," he said, "I thought I might have stepped in something outside and didn't want to cart it up there."

Nikki dropped the broom brush against the floor, still clutching the handle tightly. "You didn't hear me calling?"

"No. I heard you singing, though. You have a nice voice."

All calm, as if no discomfort existed between them. As if his sudden appearance wasn't quite the surprise. She could see by his face the first was an effort and the second not even recognized.

"I'm pretty sure your brother is in the house," she said to him.

"I know."

"Is there—do you need—" she stuttered, searching for a polite way to ask him why he was in the barn, but the structure, the property, did belong to his brother, after all, and he had every right to be wherever he pleased. She decided to stop floundering and ask him straight out. "Why are you here?"

"To lend a hand. Didn't Luke tell you?"

Nikki stepped back from the open stairhead as Rory started to climb. She returned the broom to where she had found it. "No," she said when his head, his upper body appeared. He paused.

"Odd," Rory said. "When he suggested I come by, I figured he'd either cleared it with you or at least would have mentioned it. He seems to think I need involvement with the holidays this year."

Nikki observed him climb the remaining steps into the loft. "Like Charlie Brown?" she said, referring to the beloved, long-ago Christmas special that she still watched yearly.

Rory's head cocked momentarily to the side. "What? Oh, yes, I suppose so."

"It worked for good ol' Charlie Brown."

"If I recall correctly, it was a rather painful transition for him and he only got to the joyful part with the unanticipated help of his so-called friends."

"Yep," said Nikki, turning back to her brush and the unpainted crate, "that's the way it often happens. I'm thinking Mr. Schulz got it right."

Rory said nothing. Nikki glanced back at him. He got his expression under control, looked from side to side across the workbench.

"Is there another brush?"

"I wasn't expecting anyone," Nikki said, "so, no."

He reached around behind him, whipping one out from his back pocket. "I came prepared, just in case."

Although not exactly chipper, Rory did seem to be trying for a more light-hearted approach. Even pretending sometimes helped to alter one's mood. Not always, but sometimes. Nikki had used that tactic more than once herself in recent weeks.

Laying down the brush again, Nikki spread out some more newspaper. Rory grabbed another crate and set it down nearby. "Thanks," he said.

"Thank you," she countered. "The help is appreciated." Nikki reached for the radio, hovered over the volume button with her forefinger. "Music okay?"

His hesitation was fractional. If she hadn't been looking straight at him, she would have missed it.

"Sure," he said. "Music is fine."

Before long, Nikki was singing again as they painted through the next two boxes. In her early twenties, she'd taken part in a few local theater productions, followed by on and off caroling stints. The love of song had never left her. Rory, however, had not joined in. Not everyone liked to sing or accompany others. Still, she finally shot him a quick look.

"What's wrong?" she asked.

"Nothing. My wife used to sing."

"Should I stop?"

"Not at all. I'm just listening. That's okay, right?"

"Yes, I'm a bit of a ham when it comes to that, so listening is no problem. I sang out, as my mom used to call it. She did, as well. Performing, you know? Just local stuff."

"Kat was in the choir. She liked it, too."

Nikki slid the paintbrush back and forth across the wood. "I bet this was a busy time of year for her."

"It was. A lot of practices and appearances in different places around the state. They were that good."

His voice sounded normal, lightly animated, maybe even happy in memory. As it should be. These were nice things to remember. Things that had been important to his wife and likely to them both.

"Did she have a favorite?" Nikki asked, and realized in his silence she might have gone too far. But when she glanced aside at him, she saw he was remembering, deciding, not mourning.

"*Ava Maria*," he said.

"My mom, too. Her voice was so much richer and had more range than mine." She left it at that, left it for him to bring up whatever he wished, and returned to her painting. They had both moved well into the next two crates when he spoke again.

"She like *I Wonder as I* Wander, too. I haven't been to see the church choir's Christmas performance since."

"I didn't listen to any version of *Ave Maria* for a couple years, myself," Nikka said. "I do now, though. I understand where you are, but don't let too much time pass. You'll have lost not only your wife, but yourself. I don't think she'd want that."

The brush stilled in his hand. "You don't know me."

"You're right. Not well, anyway. But I know grief. Everyone knows grief. I'm not belittling it when I say so. Remember Charlie Brown."

"That was just a cartoon."

"Not just a cartoon," said Nikki. "The message was real and powerful. Why do you think it still resonates? We're all in the same boat. We need something to believe in, something that gives us hope. And we need friends. I'd say you have the first and last, but maybe have lost sight of the middle thing."

He grunted. She half-expected him to leave. He kept right on painting alongside her. In silence, yes, but she felt no sad or angry vibes from him. He'd just gone quiet. She was okay with quiet. She liked quiet herself, oddly enough. Sometimes she sang into it on purpose, though. Because there could be echoes in that quiet. No doubt, Rory listened to his own now.

With the last crate painted, Rory plucked the brush from Nikki's hand. "I'll take these down to the sink and wash them and you can clean up the rest up here?"

"Sure."

Painting had been a non-messy endeavor, surprisingly, and took no time at all to clear. Locating a mallet, Nikki hammered the lid shut on the paint's remains and then headed down the stairs with the can. Rory came out from a back room swinging water from the brushes in his hands. He held out hers.

"Thank you," Nikki said. "Again. You've been a huge help in all this."

He shrugged. "Luke also informs me I am to take all the crates and the trees to Hannah's when you're ready. Well, he asked, really, and I said yes. Just let me know when."

Nikki nodded with another thanks. Rory stepped outside. She shut off the lights at the bank of switches on the barn wall. Rory waited for her to step outside before pushing shut the barn door, latching it, and putting the lock in place. Nikki returned the nearly empty paint can to her trunk.

"You know, your brother told me to come up to the house if I had any trouble with the door. Was he not expecting you?"

"He had his doubts, I'm sure," said Rory, heading toward his truck.

"But you came."

"Yep. Maybe I figured it was time I did get involved with…things again."

Nikki smiled. "A Charlie Brown Christmas."

"Shut up," he said, his lips quirked into something resembling amusement. He climbed into his truck and backed out, turned the vehicle around and drove to the road below where he waited, it seemed, until she'd safely gotten into her car and was headed home as well.

Chapter Nine

Nikki's phone rang as she headed out from the hardware store parking lot the next morning. She'd run in for picture wire and hooks, something she'd need for hanging the large pictures once they arrived. Depressing the button on her steering wheel, she answered Tessa's call.

"We have a delivery," Tessa said, rather gleefully. "I thought you might want to come over and check it out."

Nikki went straight over. She met Tessa in the woman's office and together they strolled down to the basement level. Large boxes had been propped against the shelves. With a utility knife, Nikki carefully cut them open, pulling out the canvases printed with Connor Falls' most recognizable architecture. She lined them against more shelves and the nearest wall.

"They look great," Tessa said, her hands

clasped together beneath her chin.

Nikki had to admit Tessa was right. The enlargements did look great. Exactly as Nikki had envisioned. She just might be pulling this down-to-the-wire display thing together after all.

The last box contained all the prints for the wooden cutouts. Nikki glanced through those with Tessa oohing and aahing at her shoulder. Nikki restored them to their packaging and set the box aside to take home. After, she walked from one canvas to the next, eyeing the large canvases up and down for any defect and finding none.

"I'll need to send Sean a Christmas gift. He got these done and to me way ahead of the promised time. I didn't expect them until tomorrow, and even then, I thought they might not be here until Wednesday."

"This works out well, doesn't it? I'd decided at closing time tomorrow, I'd have some of my people strip the windows and block them from outside view with the drapes. That way, you can work in the evening, if you wish, or through the day on Wednesday or however you want to do it. No one's in on Thanksgiving, of course, but the display will be ready for everyone to see." At Nikki's raised eyebrows, she added, "We still close on Thanksgiving, Christmas, New Year and Easter. I know, old-fashioned, but no one complains. We haven't experienced any crushing financial repercussions from continuing the tradition. It's expected now."

"Wow," was all Nikki could say.

Tessa smiled. "So, you should have time to finish everything for Black Friday morning without having to rush, yes?"

Nikki was touched. "Definitely. That's very kind of you. And much appreciated."

"Well, this is all last minute. You deserve some concession."

After returning the canvases to the cushioned packaging, Nikki carried the smaller ones and the box of photos to be affixed on the wood cutouts to her car. The list of which shop owner received which smaller canvas had been left at the cottage. She needed to print out the invoices anyway, to be delivered along with the items to each store. In the Jefferson's driveway, she found Rory in conversation with Sheila. Not wanting to disturb an obviously intense exchange, Nikki pulled her car in as close to the cottage as possible, got out, and proceeded to carry everything inside. During the process, she could hear them both. Not the words, but the tone. Neither appeared angry, however. Something else was in the wind. Whatever it might be, Rory stood like a man not ready to back down. From what, Nikki couldn't figure. It really had nothing to do with her, though. She didn't need to know.

After carrying the last package inside, Nikki headed back out again. She'd forgotten the grocery store. She passed Rory and his former mother-in-law still in earnest converse and waved, making sure they understood by the gesture she didn't intend to interrupt them. She had no idea what could bring such a rebellious expression to a grown man's face, but she wasn't about to stop and find out.

Realizing that to make something for Thanksgiving dinner, whether dessert or a side, she'd have to buy everything from the ingredients to measuring cups, bowls, utensils, she opted to load up on staples for meals for a few days and stop at Gina's bakery instead for a special surprise. If Sheila had ordered anything, Gina would know, and Nikki could pick something else entirely.

It seemed everyone else possessed the same plan to purchase baked goods. Nikki maneuvered her way to the back of the line to patiently await her turn. Recognizing she couldn't hold Gina up with questions, Nikki made a decision to get a cookie tray and spent her time peering around customers to gain some idea what assortment to choose. When she got to the counter, Gina was smiling as usual. Nikki didn't understand how the woman maintained her cool in such madness.

"Nikki, hi. What can I get for you?"

"The Jeffersons have invited me for Thanksgiving dinner. The cottage kitchen isn't equipped for making anything, so I thought maybe a cookie tray. Do you know what they like?"

"Gingerbread," Gina answered without hesitation. "We've been doing house-shaped gingerbread cookies. You could pick up a fresh batch Wednesday afternoon. I'll set aside—how many?"

"A dozen of those and a dozen of whatever else you think would work. Do you want me to pay you now?"

Gina shook her head. "Nope. Catch me when you come back for them. So," she went on, as if the store wasn't packed behind Nikki, "Thanksgiving with the Jeffersons. That'll be nice."

"I'm looking forward to it. I'm thinking I should get out of the way, though, and not take up any more of your time?"

"Thanks. Will you still be here next week?"

Nikki nodded. "Through the end of the year. I've decided to stick around."

"Have you?" Gina responded with another broad smile and a distinct twinkle in her dark brown eyes. "Let's get together for coffee or something next week, then, okay?"

"I would love to," said Nikki, and squeezed her way toward the door. Outside in the chill air, she drew a deep breath. Coming back into town tomorrow would be perfect. She'd make sure to allow enough time to deliver the canvases and invoices, saving Gina's for last. Today, she needed to hurry back to the cottage to trim and adhere all the photos to the wood. Shoving up her coat sleeve, she spun on her heel with an eye to her watch, and plowed right into a large body standing several feet from her on the sidewalk.

"Sorry! Sorry, I—oh. Rory."

He looked barely ruffled by the collision.

"Were you just in the bakery?"

"Yes. I was getting some cookies to bring to Thanksgiving dinner."

"Thanksgiving dinner? With who?"

He sounded surprised, possibly wondering who would have invited her in a town full of strangers. Yet, not everyone was a stranger. Not anymore.

"The Jeffersons," Nikki said. "Sheila invited me." She heard the breath rush from his lungs and frowned. "Something wrong?"

He glanced toward From the Hart's opening door and its jangling bell. "Nope. What did you get? Just so I can make sure I don't order the same thing."

It hadn't occurred to her Rory would be there. If she had considered it at all, she had assumed he'd be with his brother or some other family member. "Cookies. Gina knows which ones. She'll steer you straight."

He nodded and without looking at her again made his way into the bakery, sidestepping the people mingled inside. Nikki didn't quite realize she had continued to watch him until he turned and their eyes met. She looked away before he did. Odd, her shying away and not him. But she supposed this could be viewed as progress on his part.

And what was it on hers? Nothing. The whole meeting had been awkward. She had a lot on her mind and on her plate. Time to get back home.

Home. She had been thinking about the

cottage in those terms since she decided to stay in Connor Falls through the holidays. Climbing into her car, she knew she really had to stop doing that.

*   *   *

Rory's gaze didn't leave Nikki's retreating form until she'd disappeared from sight. For some reason, he found himself remembering the way she had laughed at the party in Manhattan. Frequently and whole-heartedly. She hadn't been drunk. Far from it. She'd only had a drink or two the entire night before switching over to soda, then water. She hadn't been flirting with him, either. Hadn't acted as if she expected him to accompany her back to her room. She had been, quite honestly, an independent force among so many conflicting signals elsewhere, as if she didn't really give a fig what anyone thought of her or her reasons for being there. Had concerns about nothing except, perhaps, the prolonged conversation with him. No underlying agenda. Maybe that was why he had relaxed his guard. The pain, the grief hadn't left him, but they seemed to settle elsewhere for those few hours. Still part of him, but not the end of him.

Shortly, at Thanksgiving dinner with his former in-laws, he'd be spending time with her again. Not like they had working together in Pete's barn and Luke's, but in a social gathering. A family gathering. He exhaled.

Sheila would not be happy if he backed out.

He had a feeling Kat would not have been too thrilled with him either.

Chapter Ten

The noon sun felt warm on Rory's head. Warmer than the past three days, at any rate. Rummaging through his toolbox, he caught movement along the path from the cottage. Nikki, heading his way, getting ready to corner him by his truck. Well, not cornering exactly. She merely walked up to him, squinting in the sun.

"Hi. Could I have your brother's phone number?"

Rory straightened. "Sure. Cell or landline?"

"Does he have both?" Nikki asked in surprise. "Whichever he's most likely to answer."

Rory gave her Luke's cell number, knowing he'd be in the barn or the fields, and watched her enter the digits into her contacts.

"Everything has arrived," she said. "Luke told me to let him know when I would need the trees and crates at Hannah's. I know you said he volunteered you to help with that. In fact, he told me he was volunteering you. But it doesn't seem fair. You have work to do. I'll see if anyone can point me in the direction of a person who I might hire to lend a hand. Otherwise, I feel I'm taking advantage."

"It's fine," he said.

"Your brother must have extra help during the holiday season. Perhaps one of them has some time tomorrow—"

"I'm free tomorrow," he blurted. "I'll do it."

Nikki stared up at him, her phone clutched in her hand. "Rory, I don't—"

"What time?"

Her eyebrow arched. One eyebrow. He watched it lift with a self-conscious fascination. He didn't know how a person physically managed the mechanics. She shifted her weight from her right foot to the left.

"First thing, I guess," Nikki said. "As soon as the store opens. They're blocking the windows after closing tonight so no one can see in. I might get started tonight though. Tessa said I could. The big canvases are already in the basement. They got delivered yesterday."

"What time tonight?" he heard himself ask. Honestly, he had nothing going on. Not tonight, not any night.

The eyebrow lowered in the opposite direction. "What?"

He reached for her phone, which remained open to the contact screen. "What time tonight? It wouldn't hurt to have an extra pair of hands. And let me give you my number, too, in case plans change."

She bit her lip, letting him have her cell. He entered his info into her contacts, handed the phone back. She glanced at it before shoving it into her coat pocket.

"Thank you. Maybe around eight? Before the store closes. I'm not sure what the arrangement will be to get out of there and lock up afterward, though. Maybe they have an exit that's not alarmed if you go out not in. At any rate, the canvases need to be prepped before they are put in the windows with fasteners and wires for hanging. I do appreciate this, Rory."

"It's the Charlie Brown thing," he said.

Smiling, she started walking backward toward her car. "I've got deliveries in town right now, to several of the business owners who ordered smaller versions of what's going to be in Hannah's windows. I'll be seeing the others tomorrow. I wonder if I'm going to have to fit them up for hanging, too? I mean, it's not my responsibility to do so for everyone, but I'll gladly take care of—" She stopped, eyes widening as if in memory. "Crud."

"Let me guess," he said. "No drill?"

She released a quick breath. "No. It burned up in the fire. Or melted, or whatever plastic and metal tend to do when engulfed in flame."

His mouth opened. She hadn't mentioned any fire. Yet, why would she? He never asked how her life had progressed since that evening years before. Their recent conversations had been vague or general or else about him and his loss. He took a step toward her. "You weren't…was anyone hurt?"

"No, everyone got out unharmed. But it was a total loss of property for anyone with an apartment at the heart of it."

"And you?"

She jerked a thumb over her shoulder toward her car. "What I had with me in the back seat and trunk when I arrived here is it. I replaced some things right away. I had to for my business, and because naturally I needed clothes and a toothbrush, but as far as the furniture and all, renter's insurance hasn't paid out yet. I've been assured they will but there's a holdup due to the report."

"They think someone might have set it?"

Nikki shrugged. "I don't know."

He stared at her for a full second in silence.

"Well, I have to get going." She started backing away again.

"I have one," he said.

"One what?"

"A drill."

She lifted a hand, shook her head. "I'll buy a drill from Pete."

The easy way she said his once-father-in-law's name made Rory wince. He reached into the open toolbox in the truck bed, yanked out the drill and the bits in their cases, held them out. "Here. I'm not afraid of you running off with it."

Reluctant, yet with a grateful thank you, she took the two cases from him.

"Call me when you're ready to head over to the store," he said.

"All right." She hurried to her car and left.

Her 'all right' hadn't sounded quite definite. He

had a feeling she might not call him at all. Realizing his inner voice had taken on an insecure whine and that he had probably lost his ability in the past couple years to read the simplest statement, he returned to work.

Coincidentally, when Nikki pulled back into her parking space hours later, he was in the exact same spot doing the exact same thing as before, shifting tools around in the box. It ended up he had needed his drill, after all. Fortunately, he still carried around the hand-crank version. The simpler, non-electric tool served its purpose quite well and had worked for what needed doing.

"How'd everything go?" he called out to her.

Her steps lagged as she carried his electric drill and bits toward the truck. She snorted a tired laugh. "Fine. People like to talk a lot around here, don't they?"

"They do. Sometimes it's all a bit much, but really, they're being social."

"I know." She placed the cases onto the truck bed. "It just made everything take longer than anticipated."

He curved his mouth at her, not quite a smile. "Better than silence, though."

She returned his gaze in understanding and nodded slowly. "Better than silence."

Following another thanks, she headed toward the cottage. She'd gotten about halfway there when he spoke again. "Do you have time for dinner?"

She answered over her shoulder without missing a step. "I certainly hope so."

He could have let it go there. He wasn't sure

why he didn't. Well, part of him knew. Part of him understood that what he would say next was okay. So, he did.

"With me, I mean."

She stopped, turned, gazed back at him.

"We both need to go into town to Hannah's," he hurried on, "and, quite frankly, I'm sick of peanut butter sandwiches. I've been lax with the grocery shopping."

"We don't both need to go to Hannah's," she reminded him.

"I said I'd help, and I will. It's not a date," he added, even though his stomach churned like it was, like he'd become a high school kid again, "just a matter of convenience. We can leave straight from here and stop by Luke's to at least grab the crates, then eat."

She hesitated. He figured he knew why. Since her arrival, he had made it clear on more than one occasion, or as clear as he could manage, that he wanted to be left alone. Except he didn't. Not right now, anyway. She probably recognized his effort to be social, though, no matter how temporary, because she quietly agreed.

"On one condition, though," she added.

Uh-oh.

"I pay."

His shoulders jerked. "What? No. I asked you, so I—"

"I owe you, Rory. For all you've done, it's the least I can do."

"I'm not finished yet. You can get the bill next time."

He dismissed any argument by gathering up the returned cases to place inside the tool box. Only when she responded in agreement before walking away did he realize what he had said.

Next time.

*　　*　　*

Nikki picked up her brush to subdue the curly brown tangle caused by a day's running around and put it back down on the sink edge. Surely, Rory would notice if she tamed her hair and might think she'd primped herself for him. But honestly, she would take the time to control her crazy hair for anyone's public view. Grabbing the brush again, she gave a few quick strokes to the strands, dampened her hands after, and smoothed the staticky mass down.

"There," she said to her image in the mirror. "That'll do."

A light knock sounded on the outside door.

"Coming!"

Nikki retrieved her coat and purse on the way, yanking the door open without asking who it was, something she would not have in the apartment complex. Not that she was overly paranoid or didn't trust her neighbors. It just wasn't done.

"Hi," she said, spotting Rory standing in the light thrown by the solar fixture on the nearby lamppost. She strode outside shoving her arms into her coat sleeves. He took a single step back, away from her flailing arms, reached past her and yanked the door closed. She looked at him sidelong. "Are you still okay with doing this?"

"Sure," he said. Nikki couldn't read his tone, but decided to take it at face value.

"Great. Let's go." She led the way to his truck and reached for the door handle.

"Wait!"

Anticipating a change of heart, Nikki backed away from the truck door. He hurried past her and pulled it open, bending to remove some things from the floor and seat, stowing them on the floor behind. Straightening, he pulled the door wide, sweeping his hand in indication she could get in.

"I haven't had anyone in there for a while," he said, shutting the door after she had seated herself.

The truck's interior didn't smell quite the way she thought a man's personal work vehicle might, especially when it hadn't seen other occupants for some time. Instead, it smelled like him, like his soap or shampoo's light fragrance, a scent which had wriggled its way into unconscious recognition somewhere along the line. Rory climbed in behind the wheel, started the truck, and gave her a funny little nod before backing out.

"Luke's first, right?"

"Yes," Nikki answered, having called Rory's brother. Luke had seemed a bit thrown by the fact she would be arriving with Rory, but had recovered nicely enough to say he'd have hot cocoa waiting, courtesy of his daughter. A daughter standing by him when they pulled up, jumping up and down in her pink coat. She ran straight to Rory as soon as he stepped out from the truck and hugged him before giving Nikki a huge wave. Nikki waved back, delighted.

"I've had an idea," said Luke. "A slight change of plans. Nikki, could you hang around with Lyddie for a little while? Frank had to leave, so I'll help Rory with the trees and crates and he and I can take them over to the store. I happened to talk to Tessa earlier, and she said the trees and all can be put directly into the enclosed courtyard out back for a short time."

Nikki exchanged a look with Rory. Her stomach growled.

Rory cleared his throat. "Nikki and I were going to grab dinner on the way into town."

If Luke had looked any more shocked, he would have resembled a cartoon. He recovered quickly and well, however. "I didn't know," he said.

"It's all right," said Nikki. "We'll work it out. I'm happy to spend some time with Lydia in exchange for not lugging balled trees around. Later, I'll have to, of course, but I won't complain about not doing it twice."

Lydia's eyes hadn't left her uncle since he'd spoken. "You're going…on a date?"

"No," said Nikki and Rory in unison, "it's not a date."

"It's just dinner," Nikki explained.

"For convenience," Rory added. "We're both hungry."

Lydia turned, cocked her head at her dad. He squeezed the small hand curled in his. "Whatever," he whispered.

"Luke," Rory said. "Don't."

Luke had the grace to look guilty. Nikki went

over to him and extended her own gloved hand to Lydia's. "What are we going to do while they're gone?"

"Um, I dunno. I can show you Uncle Rory's pictures on our wall and then, maybe, we can watch television?"

"You have homework, Lyddie," said Luke.

"Oh, yeah. Right. That. I'll get it done, Dad. You know I will."

Luke sighed. "Don't I, just? I'm not sure why I even bother to remind you." He winked at her, bent and kissed her on the head. Immediately after, the two men headed into the barn and Lydia pulled Nikki toward the house. Inside, a fire burned on the fireplace grate, filling the air with warmth. Something simmered on the stove, fragrant and making Nikki's stomach growl again. Lydia brought Nikki to the fireplace wall and began an enthusiastic and lengthy explanation regarding each enlarged, framed photograph hanging there. Nikki noted the obvious indications these were Rory's work, from composition to the special quality of light.

"Your Uncle Rory's very talented," Nikki said.

"Do you like him?"

Oh. Blunt child. "We don't know each other very well, but he is my friend. I think. Starting to be, anyway."

"He's been sad a long time."

"So, I've heard," Nikki answered quietly.

"Do you…do you know what happened?"

Nikki thought a moment about how to respond and finally asked, "Do you?"

"She died. Aunt Kat did. Uncle Rory's wife. She was sick. Dad explained it to me. He's good about that. Dad doesn't treat me like I shouldn't know things."

"Yes, I can tell you're a very grown-up young girl."

"I don't like seeing Uncle Rory so sad."

"I'm sure you don't." Nikki kept silent on the fact she didn't like seeing him so sad, either. She barely knew him, after all. Bu since sympathy was allowed for absolute strangers, there was really no reason she couldn't be permitted the sentiment for someone she was getting to know better.

"If you're hungry," Lydia said, "we have some leftovers. We ate early tonight."

Something about the way Lydia uttered the last made Nikki wonder how unusual an occurrence early dinner might be. "I'm good, thanks. I'll wait. Unless my stomach starts to growl a lot more. Then I might have to sneak a little bite."

Lydia giggled and ran around the couch to grab the television remote. She plopped down on a cushion and smacked the one next to her in invite. "I don't watch the news. Do you?"

"Not if I can help it," Nikki admitted, taking the seat beside her.

Snuggling into the sofa back, Lydia turned on what appeared to be a show on home décor. Strange choice for a child, Nikki thought, until she saw it had something to do with decorating the house for Christmas. They settled in to watch, Lydia providing occasional commentary. Abruptly, the front door opened.

"Hey, pumpkin," Luke addressed his daughter. "Get your coat back on. We'll follow Uncle Rory and Nikki into town to help unload so they can—"

"Go on their date?" Lydia finished.

"It's not a date," Nikki said, without much effect. Lydia gave her a *sure it isn't* look. Outside, Nikki climbed back into the passenger seat in Rory's truck.

"Sorry about that," he said.

"About what?"

"Having our plans waylaid."

"It's fine. I appreciate the help. Yours, too."

Rory pulled out onto the road heading into town. "Yeah, but…"

"But?"

He shrugged. "Nothing."

Nikki studied Rory's profile a moment in the dashboard lights. "It's fine, Rory," she said again. The remaining trip passed in silence, Nikki looking out the window at the shadowed scenery and Rory frowning at the headlight-illuminated road. Twice he opened his mouth to say something, and both times shut his lips without speaking.

"It's okay," Nikki said.

"What's okay?"

"Whatever you're feeling."

"How do you know what I'm feeling?" he asked, turning a corner in town to park the truck in Hannah's back lot.

"I don't. I'm just saying, whatever you're feeling is okay. There's no rule book for loss, you know."

Maneuvering the truck close to an area closed

off by cement block, he muttered, "Sometimes I wish there was."

Nikki grunted. "Can you imagine how many volumes would exist to address the needs of every individual? Each person is different. Every single one of us."

Rory put the truck in park, folded his hands over the wheel, bowed his dark head. "I know."

"Look, your brother will be here any second. Be pleased about that, if nothing else. I'd considering giving my right arm for one of those. I have no siblings."

Rory threw open the door and jumped down onto the blacktop. He looked back in at her. "You're right. You're absolutely right. Do you want to run into the store and let somebody know we're here dropping off the trees?"

Nikki gave him a thumbs up and hustled inside to advise the evening manager. She also told the young man she'd be back later to start work on the windows. She figured she would find out the particulars then about lights and exiting the store. By the time she returned to the back lot, Luke and Rory were unloading Rory's pickup. Lydia sat watching from the open door of her father's truck, legs swinging. She waved at Nikki as she arrived. Unwilling to not do her share, Nikki grabbed several crates. Lydia appeared at her side, arms out for one. Within fifteen minutes, the truck bed stood empty except for the attached toolbox.

"You've been so helpful and so kind," Nikki said, breath frosting in the cold air. "I can't thank you all enough."

"No problem," answered Luke, sliding a look at his brother. "We'll, uh, leave you to it, then."

Conscious of the limited space between her shoulder and Rory's arm, Nikki watched Luke drive away, presumably heading home. "Sweet kid," said Nikki about Lydia. "Smart. Bit of a character."

"Agreed," said Rory. "Let's get some dinner." He started walking away from the truck, glancing back at her when she didn't follow.

Nikki studied him a second. "Here in town?"

"Sure," he said. "Why not?"

"I thought you didn't do things like that."

"Like eat?"

"Like…be around other people. People you know."

"Oh." He shifted his weight from one foot to the other. "I'm trying, Nikki. It's time I did, I think. Come on. There's a small restaurant not far from here. It's a casual place. I promise we're not underdressed for it," he added with a rare smile. Seeing his mouth turn up in genuine amusement, she smiled herself.

Side by side, they crossed over at the corner and continued down the main street. Nikki pointed out the canvases in the shop fronts, explaining the larger versions would appear in Hannah's windows.

"Once we're sitting down," Rory said, "remind me to ask you about your life since that other time, would you? I haven't asked a single question. I should have. I've been too wrapped up in my own head for too long, I guess."

"Ask me now," said Nikki.

"What?"

"Ask me something now. Anything you want."

"Okay. What happened to that boyfriend of yours? I'm assuming he's not in the picture, or you wouldn't be spending the holidays here in Connor Falls."

Nikki paused on the sidewalk. "I don't remember telling you that."

"About the boyfriend, or the holidays in Connor Falls?"

"Both, I guess."

"Sheila told me about the holidays. You told me about…what was his name?"

Nikki glanced down at the concrete between her booted feet. "Ted. And yeah, he's not in the picture. For some time now. Is that really the first question that came to mind?"

Rory touched her arm to keep her walking, quickly letting go. "Oddly," he said, "yes."

Nikki's lips twisted, wondering at the implication. "Okay, then. May I ask you something now?"

He didn't answer, nodding in silence only after several seconds had passed.

"If it snows while I'm here, would you possibly take the time to give me a few pointers on how you get the light so perfect in a photo? I'm assuming it's more than just timing."

A muscle in his jaw twitched. "That's the question popping into your head?"

"Oddly," she said, mimicking his words, "yes."

He let out a long breath. "I don't take photos any more, Nikki. I told you that."

"You don't have to take. Just teach."

He stopped short. Nikki wondered if he'd had enough. He raised his hand, moved it past her, reaching, she realized for the handle on a door to a small restaurant called Shelly's.

"We're here," he said. "And okay. I'll do it. If it snows."

Chapter Eleven

I'll do it if it snows.

That sounded like a promise he didn't mean to keep. Felt like it, anyway, and yet a part of him truly wanted to. Wanted a camera back in his hands, as well, framing images, creating something from what he saw through the lens. As Rory ate his meal, he pictured the season's first snowfall. Snow was not unknown even in November in this area, sometimes surprisingly heavy. Between now and the New Year, snow might, indeed, fall.

Rory glanced at Nikki as she ate and chatted about her plans for Hannah's windows, what items would go in, the impression she hoped it would make on the townspeople. She wanted what they saw to make them happy, this stranger in his town.

His lips curled at her enthusiasm. He brought up the logistics for what she intended. How he thought the canvases might be hung, reminded her about the need for store help to keep the trees watered, possibly lining the crates with trash bags to insure nothing leaked. When the check came, he grabbed it. Nikki made a quick objection, and then thanked him. Exiting Shelly's small eatery, they headed back to the department store.

Nikki continued talking. Not non-stop. She paused in between sentences for thought and for him to respond with more than a grunt or a yes or no. He answered, still lost in thought about his commitment to 'teach' her. It wouldn't be a big deal. He knew it wouldn't. Just an exchange of knowledge. He'd done that, instructing small classes at the community college at night for a time before…well, before. Everything seemed to be before. Before had been life, after had become nothing more than going through the motions.

"Nikki."

She glanced up at him.

"I didn't really ask you anything about you while we ate, did I?"

"No, but that's okay. I think you've got the picture anyway. Boyfriend gone, with the assumption of no significant other to follow, since I'm here on my own. Fire. Stuff burned up. Job, still the same. Something missing you'd like to know?"

The question came without sarcasm. So, he asked, "Are you happy?"

She blinked, her long lashes lowering and lifting again. "Sure I am."

"I remember how hard you laughed that night."

"Well, I still do. Maybe not as often."

"Me, either."

"I noticed," she said.

"Yes," he said, "I know."

She shot him an apologetic look. "I'm trying not to be obvious."

"It's okay. A portion of me recognizes it's time

I came back to life. The rest of me has trouble caring whether I do or don't."

"I saw the self-help book on the shelf in the cottage. Did that aid you at all?"

He shrugged. "It did make me recognize healing has to come from the inside."

Nikki made a noise in her throat. Agreement, he thought. "It helps not to be alone, too. Loneliness is a killer. Good thing you have family, yours and hers."

"And friends," he said.

She threw a sideways smile in his direction. "And friends."

They reached Hannah's and went inside, a little too early for closing and the draped windows, so headed into the basement instead after checking in with Tessa. Nikki pulled some diagrams from her bag and showed them to him.

"You're thorough," he said.

"I try."

"When are they putting the merchandise in?"

"Tomorrow night? Surely, before Thanksgiving morning."

"Hannah's isn't open on Thanksgiving. It's a longstanding tradition. They close the entire day."

Nikki nodded. "Right. Tessa told me. But she wants the windows finished so people can see them, even though the store is closed. You know what it's like to me, being here in Connor Falls?"

"No," he said. "What?"

"It's a little like stepping back in time. Not my time. Just time in general."

"Is there anything wrong with that?"

Nikki shook her head. "Not at all. Let's reopen these boxes and take the canvases back out." She pulled a marker from her bag. "I'm going to mark the frames on the backs with a number coinciding with the drawings I made."

From that minute on, Nikki became focused on the work at hand. Rory followed her lead, somewhat relieved discussion had moved away from a personal level. Once the store closed and the heavy draperies had been pulled across to conceal the windows, they started lugging everything inside for positioning, starting with the trees. They worked together well and almost silently, transforming the blank space into something which would upon completion be an almost magical complement to the town itself.

"It looks great," Rory said quietly, standing a little away, his back against the heavy curtain.

Nikki smiled, glanced at her watch, and gasped. "Is it really that late?"

"Yep."

"I'm sorry. You have work in the morning."

"So do you."

"Yeah, but—"

"No buts. I volunteered, remember?"

Nikki spun to face him. A dark smudge marred her nose and one cheek. He found himself fascinated by it and forced himself to look away. There would be no fascination here.

"Look, Rory, about that. I can't expect you to do all of this for nothing. I would be paying someone else."

"No," he said, bringing his gaze back to her

face. "No," he repeated. "I didn't agree to do this with an expectation of payment. I'm not really sure why I agreed except, with a little prodding from my former in-laws, I recognized it would be good for me. Okay? Let's leave it at that."

She opened her mouth, likely engaged in a mental debate about letting the matter drop, then clamped her lips shut again and nodded. "All right. But I'm going to do something. You might find a mysterious box showing up on your doorstep."

"You don't know my address."

Nikki crossed her arms, cocked her head a little to the side, lips curling, the smudges on her skin catching the overhead light like shadows. "In this town, I'm sure I only have to ask."

"Don't," he said. "Please. Give me this, would you?"

She sobered. "Of course. Whatever you need."

"Thanks."

"Great, then. That's settled. I think we're done here for the night. I only have a little more to do tomorrow." Nikki headed for the small door providing exit from the bank of windows. She attempted to turn the knob, pushed on the door, and pushed again. Eyes wide, she turned to face him. "These aren't supposed to lock, are they?"

"I don't know." Stepping past her, Rory gave the tiny knob a shake. The door didn't budge. "Jammed, maybe?"

"I hope not." Nikki shoved the door again, grabbed the knob, twisted it to no avail. She smacked the panel with her palm. "This can't happen."

Rory noted a slight panic in her voice. "Are you okay? You're not claustrophobic, are you?"

She pointed to several empty water bottles on the floor. "I drank all those. You know what that means, don't you?"

"Um…yes." His mouth twisted, biting back a laugh. She shot him a withering look. His laughter broke free, echoing in the enclosed space, harder and louder than it had in a long time. Somehow, he couldn't stop. When she stamped her foot, he nearly doubled over.

"It's not funny."

"I know," he gasped.

She clutched her abdomen. "Don't. Make. Me. Laugh." Too late. They both stood beneath the low window ceiling chortling like fools. Suddenly, the small door opened.

"Tessa!" Rory cried, spotting the woman's face in the shadows beyond. She stared back at him, brows arched, no doubt puzzled by his present demeanor. Not surprising. Although better friends with Kat than with him, she'd witnessed his crushing grief on more than one occasion since Kat's passing. A lot of folks hereabout had.

Slowly, her mouth curled up. "Good to hear you laughing, Rory. What on earth is going on?"

"We couldn't get out," Nikki said.

"Oh, yes, this doorknob malfunctions sometimes. I've been meaning to get it fixed."

"What are you doing here at this hour?" Rory asked.

Tessa rolled her eyes. "Working. Paperwork. My favorite."

"Good thing you were here." Nikki bent and gathered up the empty bottles for the recycling. "I really have to, well, get to the ladies room."

Tessa grinned in understanding, stepping aside to let Nikki climb down and hurry past. Rory took a minute to gather up the tools, avoiding Tessa's eye.

"Rory, look at me."

Reluctantly, he did.

"You don't have to feel guilty about enjoying yourself. Everybody would be happy to see it. Everybody," she stressed.

Rory's breath rushed out. "I tell myself the same thing."

"As you should." She smiled at him, a somewhat sad, long-suffering smile, and stepped away again, waving him out from the window. "Any plans for Thanksgiving?"

"Sheila and Pete invited me," he said as he passed her and paused a few feet away.

"Good." Tessa closed and locked the door. "Taking anyone with you?"

"What?"

Tessa tipped her head toward Nikki disappearing into the restroom.

"Tessa, these are my in-laws, for crying out loud. Kat's parents. Besides, she's already going. They invited her, too. She's staying in their cottage, after all. I guess they felt sorry for her, didn't want her to be alone."

"Right. Guess so." Tessa led the way across the floor to the door to the basement and held it open for Rory. "I'll have Nikki meet you downstairs. You can go out that side door. It locks behind you and

I've already given the security company a heads up the doors aren't armed yet. I'll do it on my way out."

Rory paused with his foot on the top step, clutching the various tools in his arms. "I'm sorry for snapping at you."

"You didn't, actually. You've never been one to be snappish. But I do understand where you're coming from. It's just..."

"I know," he said, and gave her a crooked smile before descending into the storage rooms of the department store.

Nikki joined him a few minutes later. He had no idea where the inky smudges on her face had come from, yet they were gone now, scrubbed clean. Her light brown hair clung wetly to her brow and cheeks. Grabbing the two screwdrivers clamped in his left hand, she yanked open the door to the rear parking lot. White crystals glinted on the cement stairs. A thin coating only, but snow nevertheless. He glanced down at it.

"Um..."

"Don't worry," said Nikki, preceding him up the steps. "This isn't real snow. It's only a tease. When enough falls, I'll be knocking at your door for those lessons."

"You don't know where I live—"

"I told you, I can find out," she said. "Small town. Helpful people. Plus, there's always the internet."

Following her up the stairs, he chuckled. Again. If he wasn't careful, this could become habit in her company.

Chapter Twelve

The next morning, Nikki awoke with a start. She couldn't recall where she was, only saw the darkness around her, not even the light from her alarm clock on the nightstand beside her bed. A moment later she remembered. She no longer had the alarm clock, or the nightstand, or the bed.

But what she still had was good enough. More than good enough.

Nikki tossed back the blankets, swung her legs over the mattress side, shoved her feet into her new, cozy, warm slippers. She checked the time on her phone. Way too early to be up. Dawn was still an hour away. Even so, she scurried over to the window to peer outside. She half-expected to witness snow blanketed across the ground, gleaming beneath the night sky. The light coating from the night before, however, had gone, probably blown away by the wind. Too cold to melt. She thought about Rory's face, both when she'd extracted the promise from him and later, when they exited the department store basement to find snow glittering on the steps and in the parking lot. Asking him to teach her had been spur of the moment, yet in retrospect it seemed rather presumptuous and maybe even a little contrived. It hadn't been. Truly it hadn't been. She would love to learn from him. He possessed a genuine gift.

Nikki raised her eyes to the sky, to where the stars shone white and bright in the brittle air. She pulled the robe closer about her body and leaned her head against the window frame, contemplating the changes in her life. Too many to count, although the larger alterations stood out glaringly. They'd brought her here, though, to a place that gave her comfort when she hadn't thought to find any. Maybe for other reasons, too. She couldn't help but think about coincidence, about discovering the man here she'd dismissed from her mind a long time ago. A man who needed a friend separate and apart from a life filled with painful reminders.

Truthfully, though, she was one of those reminders. She figured he experienced guilt when recalling those few hours they'd spent together talking and laughing at a time when he felt he should be lost in grief. But those hours had been a reprieve, something he needed, something, perhaps, to keep him from breaking. The evening had been a simpler thing for her, she supposed. Even so, she remembered now going home to Ted, wondering why they never laughed like that anymore.

Yeah. Well. She had found out the answer to that soon enough.

Nikki turned from the window, determined to check the time on her phone, see if she might be lucky enough to catch a couple more hours' sleep. Spying movement in the field across the road, she jerked back around.

A figure strode from the field into the road and across it, right into the Jeffersons' driveway. Nikki moved to the window's side, peering out around the curtain. The figure continued toward the barn. Breaking in? But no, it went past and up to a truck parked there. Rory's truck, backed into his space. Nikki hadn't noticed the vehicle. She watched the person she now recognized as Rory pull something from his pocket. She realized it was a cell phone when the screen lit up. He gave it a quick glance, probably to check the time, then his head moved, his gaze going to the Jefferson's house before he hunched into his coat, yanked open the pickup's door, and climbed inside. He settled in, as if waiting for his workday to start, lost in thought, his gaze on the barn wall.

Okay, it would be light soon. Perhaps he'd shown up early and taken a stroll in the pre-dawn air. Or maybe he'd slept there in his truck and she hadn't known it. She hadn't heard him leave, after all. Or maybe she needed to mind her own business and not worry about Rory Hollis. Or maybe, just maybe, she should march down there and find out what was up.

Snatching her coat from the hanger, Nikki took a moment to reconsider. Only a moment. Firm in her decision, she yanked the coat on over her nightwear, which, in the cold cottage, consisted of a tee shirt, sweat shirt and flannel sleep pants, figured her slippers would serve, and headed out into the frigid darkness. She marched straight up to the truck and knocked on the passenger side window. Rory jumped, considerably more startled than she had intended.

"Sorry," she apologized in a loud whisper. He reached across, pushed the door open. She accepted it as an invitation, whether meant that way or not, and clambered up into the seat before pulling the door quietly closed.

"What are you doing awake?" he asked. Perhaps grumpily.

"Nothing. I woke up rather suddenly. You?"

"I couldn't sleep."

"So, you showed up a couple hours early for work and then went for a walk in the open air?"

"Something like that," he muttered.

"Couldn't have accomplished the last at home?"

He said nothing, compressed his lips, shook his head.

"Come inside, then. I'll make us both breakfast. Eggs and toast. Or cereal."

"I'm—"

"Not giving you a choice," she said. "If I'm going to be up before the crack of dawn, I may as well be productive."

Nikki pushed open the pickup door, stepped out and looked back in at him. He expelled a short, sharp breath.

"Fine," he said, "thank you."

"People who use the word 'fine' usually don't

mean it."

"You mean it's more like sarcasm?"

"That's the way I figure it."

"Well, I'm not being sarcastic. I'm just giving in."

"Works for me, then. Come on. It's cold out here."

Nikki preceded him to the cottage door, waiting until he caught up with her before swinging it wide and ushering him inside.

"I'll build up the fire?" he offered.

"Sure," Nikki answered, shirking off her coat. "Thanks."

While he set to work adding logs and getting them lit, Nikki prepared a quick breakfast for them both. He'd lowered himself into the camp chair near the fire. Before he could get himself detached from the deep-slung seat, Nikki handed him his plate and sat on the narrow hearth with hers.

"Thanks," he said, digging in.

Nikki waited until Rory had nearly finished eating before interrupting him. "Are you all right?" He glanced up. Nikki scooted a little away from the fire's heat. "I mean, it's an odd time to be wandering…isn't it?"

"Not for me. I don't always sleep well. I headed over early figuring I might catch a few winks in my truck, but, no."

"Well, at least you got breakfast out of it."

He offered her a crooked smile, lifted his plate from his knees. "I'll do the washing up."

Nikki stood. "Nope. Never do this minute what you can put off until later, especially dishes."

He allowed her to take his plate and utensils without argument. She placed everything in the sink and ran water into it. Behind her, she heard nothing except the crackling fire. Finally, the canvas chair creaked. The floorboard beneath her right foot dipped a little. Rory's shadow fell across the sink and the window above it as his hand lowered to the counter next to her. An abrupt fizzing warmed her blood and her skin. She refused to look at him.

"When I said we should keep in touch back then, I should have. You're a good person, Nikki."

A good person. She half expected him to pat her on the head, like a child or a dog. Good girl, Nikki. Her blood cooled. Relieved by that, she turned to face him. He stood only inches away. He stepped back. So did she, with a start, his proximity bringing on another surging reaction.

"I'm going to head over to the Jefferson's," he said. "I can sneak in through the rear door. I've done it before. I'll be able to get the day's job set up without disturbing them. Thanks for breakfast."

"No problem," Nikki said, her lips stiff.

He grabbed his coat, strode to the door, and paused there, looking back. "If you need any help later finishing up the windows, let me know, okay?"

Nikki nodded. The door closed behind him. She sat down somewhat abruptly on the nearby stairs, touched her warm cheeks, lowered her hands to her lap, clasped them together. She hadn't expected that. She wanted them to remain just friends, despite his appeal, his laugh, the charm she'd once known, the time they recently spent together. Only friends. Because anything more than friends would be too complicated considering where he was and the place she wasn't.

Rushing to the other window, the one facing the Jefferson's side yard, she peered out from behind the curtain, watching Rory round the corner toward the back door, his stride lanky, confident, despite his emotional state. For a brief instant she visualized running after him, spinning him around to face her—as if she could—and yanking him down by the coat collar to plant a generous kiss on his mouth.

Blowing out a breath, Nikki drifted over to the hearth and sat, the warmth from the fire Rory had built up hot on her back. She didn't want complication, didn't want to bring any to him either. The reprieve from life she anticipated by staying in Connor Falls through the holidays seemed to slip away. She wouldn't leave, though. She liked it too much here. She liked Rory, too, differently than she had, she supposed, a mere half hour ago. Or maybe she was lying to herself. Maybe the moment she remembered him, remembered the evening in Manhattan, something she had hidden away inside had started waving its hand like royalty in a procession.

Thanksgiving dinner with Rory and his former-in-laws could end up a big mistake.

*   *   *

After a stop at Hannah's for some last-minute adjustments and to make sure the extension cords for the lights on the trees were in place, Nikki made her way among the other shops, dropping off the remaining smaller, mounted photos for their windows. It took a lot longer than anticipated, with the owners asking for tips how to display the pieces and generally wanting to take a few minutes to talk. She'd given Rory back his drill, so was glad no one asked her for a hand putting anything up. Lastly, Nikki headed into Gina's to collect her cookie order.

"I heard about you and Rory."

Nikki looked up from her wallet with a start. "What?"

"Getting stuck in the window," Gina said, slipping the boxed cookies into a Christmas-themed bag. "Tessa happened to mention it."

"Did she now?" Nikki responded with a short, somewhat forced laugh. "It was no big deal. The door to that window apparently sticks. Good thing Tessa was still there."

"Good thing," Gina agreed, giving her a look.

"What?" Nikka asked for the second time in as many minutes. She handed Gina her credit card and grabbed the bag off the counter.

"Nothing. I'm glad Rory gave you a hand. You set yourself quite the task, but you're finished now, yes?"

"I am. And it was very nice of Rory to help me out. I think it's helping him, too."

"Oh, so you know about his history. From him, I hope?"

Nikki nodded.

"Good. He needs to talk to someone."

"Agreed," said Nikki, taking her credit card and

backing away to make room for the people lining up behind her. "Thanks for the cookies. Have a great Thanksgiving!"

"You, too," Gina answered with a wave. "Maybe we can have that cup of coffee sometime soon?"

"Sure thing. I'd like that."

Exiting the bakery, Nikki took a second to remember where she'd parked her car. She'd been crossing over Main Street enough times she'd forgotten where she'd started. Spotting her vehicle, she hurried in its direction. As soon as she got back to the Jeffersons, she'd deposit the checks she'd received from the shop owners. She didn't want to leave them sitting around in her purse or anywhere she might misplace them. The invoices all read thirty days for payment, but everyone insisted she wait while they wrote her a check. Another reason the day had gotten away from her.

Halfway down the block, she heard a familiar tune coming from her purse. Sammy's ringtone. Samantha Cook, the one close friend she'd had in Brewster. A close friend who'd moved across the country for a dream job about two months prior to the fire. Fortuitous, that. Sammy had lived in the apartment directly opposite Nikki's.

Shoving her hand into her bag, Nikki fumbled for her phone and pulled it out. "Sammy," she said, without waiting for her friend's greeting, "hi!"

"Hi, there. You sound chipper. Everything's going well in Smalltown, USA?"

"Perfect. The windows are finished. There'll be an unobtrusive unveiling early tomorrow morning."

"Good for you! And after? Where are you going next?"

"Next?" Right this moment there was no next. She hadn't mentioned to Sammy her plans to stick around Connor Falls through the holidays. That had been an on-the-spot decision. "I don't have another job lined up yet, so I—"

"Come out to Seattle! You know you want to. And after all you've been through, you could use a vacation. With me. I'll show you all the sites. We could spend Christmas together. We *should* spend Christmas together."

A week ago, Nikki would have jumped on the invite. Flown out no matter the cost. What she wanted now was to follow through with her plans, to stick around Connor Falls. To hide away? Maybe. To enjoy the peace and quiet? Certainly. To see if she could coax Rory from his grief?

This question she couldn't answer. Didn't want to answer. Refused to admit the possibility. But the fact it had popped up in her head very likely made the response a yes.

Seattle would put plenty of miles between her and the man she'd once spent a sparkling evening with. A man now broken. A man who seemed to be coming to life again.

Nikki wasn't responsible for his happiness. She knew that. But she also had to acknowledge Connor Falls was inside her now. For the first time in quite a long while, she felt at ease, almost at home. She couldn't let Rory chase her away from those feelings and couldn't let Samantha pull her away, either. She had her own demons to face down. And

Connor Falls seemed the place to do it.

"I already paid rent through the New Year," she heard herself telling Sammy. "How about just before Spring? There'd be less chance of weather issues with flying," she added.

"Are you sure?" Sammy asked after a momentary silence.

"Yes. Are you okay?"

"I'm fine," Sammy said. "To be honest, as much fun as it would be to have you out here, I'm also kind of relieved."

Nikki arched her brows at the phone. "Busy enough without me, are you?"

"No. It's just that you sound different. Better. Something happen?"

"Many things are happening," said Nikki. "It's just…a different vibe here. I think I need it."

"Then go for it," her friend responded warmly. "These next few weeks could do you a world of good. And if not, you only need to call. We can talk, or you can hop a flight. Okay?"

"Okay," Nikki agreed, smiling. "I love you, Sammy."

"Love you, too, Niks."

The call ended. Nikki realized she'd stopped dead on the sidewalk and collected herself, continuing to her vehicle, noting the streetlamps had come on, as had the white lights circling each wreath. Before Nikki reached her car, the phone rang again. She glanced at the instrument. Tessa.

"Hi, Tessa. Everything okay?"

"Where are you?"

Nikki's breath rushed out. "What's happened?"

"Nothing. Don't panic. Really. Where are you?" she asked again.

"I just left the bakery," Nikki answered, her heart pounding. She opened the car door and set the bag with the cookies on the passenger side floor. "Did the trees all fall down or something? The extension cords catch fire?"

Tessa laughed. To Nikki's rattled nerves, it didn't quite sound sincere. "Nothing bad has happened, but I need you to come see something. Could you head over to the store?"

"Yep. Will do." Nikki hung up. Her sharp panic still had not settled. Deciding it would take too long to get her car turned around, she locked the door again and started walking. Hannah's was less than a block and a half away. It wouldn't take more than five minutes.

Yet five minutes might be too long. Because people did that when they didn't want a person to lose their cool. Said it was nothing. When really, they were trying to prevent you racing into a flaming building.

Nikki picked up her feet and ran.

Chapter Thirteen

Rory wanted to bring something more than dessert to his former in-laws. How much desert did four people need? It could be a few more than four, he supposed, if Pete's sister and husband were coming. Rory had no idea. Even so, he wanted to get something especially nice for Shiela. They'd never turned their back on him, despite his lingering heartache, his prolonged and deliberate isolation. He'd acknowledged his gratitude, sure. But the time had come to acknowledge the sentiment without behaving as though it felt like a knife in his gut. Pete wouldn't want anything from Rory. Not because any harshness existed between them. For Pete, guys didn't give guys presents. But Sheila would accept it in the spirit given.

Parking near Hannah's seemed unusually sparse. Rory drove past the lot and had decided to avoid the packed side streets nearby, when something caught his eye. A crowd—a crowd for

Connor Falls, anyway—mingled on the sidewalks. He slowed his truck, looked around for some emergency. Finding nothing obvious but people waiting, he turned left and pulled his pickup into the first space he could. Puzzled, he trotted back in the store's direction.

Recognizing Tessa in the crosswalk, he hurried over to her, his eyes scanning the building for some problem. "What's going on?"

Tessa spun to look at him. "Rory, hi. I've really messed this up, haven't I?"

"Messed what up?"

"I just—"

"Tessa!"

Nikki's voice. Rory turned and found her running toward them. Rory couldn't be sure if she'd even noticed him. He was positive she hadn't when she darted in between them to address Tessa.

"What's wrong? What's happened?"

Tessa grabbed Nikki's arms, looked her straight in the eye and shook her head. "Nothing's wrong. I kind of wanted it to be a surprise, but I can see I should have told you." Stepping to the side, Tessa released an arm and swept her hand out to encompass the crowd.

"What are all these people doing here?" Nikki asked, still confused. Rory couldn't blame her. He was a bit baffled himself.

"Normally," Tessa explained, "the window displays are unveiled on Thanksgiving Eve. I figured I wouldn't be doing that this year, because of the last minute—you know. Somehow, though, the word didn't get around to everyone and these people are all here to see your display." She glanced at her watch. "We'll be opening the drapery in about five minutes and I really wanted you here front and center to see it."

Nikki's mouth twisted. "I actually hate front and center," she said quietly. "Can I just stand where I am?"

"You can," answered Tessa, "but I think you should come forward for some credit. I prepared a paragraph to read about how you stepped in and how quickly you accomplished all of this. You don't have to talk. A wave will do. I'll read my card—" She flapped it in the air, "and that'll be that, except for the oohs and aahs."

Nikki still hung back. Rory recognized a kindred reaction. When *Home* first came out, he'd been scheduled for quite a few appearances for book signings and the like. Although he'd found moments enjoyable, for the most part he would rather have been out taking more photographs. And then…

Well. And then.

He slipped his hand around Nikki's elbow. "Come on, I'll walk up there with you."

Tessa shot him a surprised look. Her lips curled up. "Good idea," she said. "You helped, too."

"Well, no," he stated, "that's not why I—"

Too late. Holding onto her note card, Tessa strode away through the crowd. Nikki raised her eyes to his. A twinkle appeared in her formerly panicked gaze.

"We could run," she stated. "Where are you parked?"

A muscle in his jaw twitched. "Not far. But I'm thinking we should just follow Tessa and suck it up."

They headed toward the store, where Tessa already appeared to be calling everyone's attention. Halfway there, he realized he still had Nikki's elbow in his grasp. Startled, he released it.

"Sorry," he mumbled.

"It's all right," she said, staring straight ahead. "I might have bolted without it."

He grunted, unsure what would be safe to say right then. Together, they reached Tessa's side, turned around to face the eager crowd on the sidewalk and in the street. Carols drifted from the building's speakers. Not loud. Rory barely heard them over the murmuring from the gathering. Tessa raised her hand. The people hushed. Lifting her card, Tessa read from it, following those few words with Nikki's introduction and then his, thanking him for his assistance. He nodded his head, noting surprise on certain faces. Those who knew him. His gaze shifted to the sidewalk at his feet.

"And now," Tessa abruptly announced, "the grand reveal."

Rory turned his back on the crowd in relief, his gaze on the covered windows. Nikki spun on her heel, too, watching the glass with her lip caught between her teeth. He could feel her nerves. He nearly reached out for her hand in reassurance, stopping himself before his arm could lift from his side. His stomach rolled. Tessa leaned forward and knocked on the nearest window signaling someone inside. She then started to count backwards from ten quite loudly, the people behind them joining in.

At 'one', hands appeared between the hangings on every window and began tugging them open. Rory watched, impressed how the store personnel managed to remain hidden behind the draped material. He realized, however, that they could have been standing out in the open and no one would have noticed. All eyes were on the displays. Accompanied by appreciative exclamations, applause filled the air.

He bent quickly toward Nikki's ear. "Good job," he whispered.

Her cheeks went rosy pink. He smelled the fresh air in her hair, and a shampoo scent. Lavender, maybe. Kat had liked lavender. He took a step away. Nikki glanced sidelong at him.

"Thanks," she said.

He shoved his hands into his coat pockets. "No problem."

Townsfolk came forward to congratulate Nikki and ask her questions, and someone from the local paper asked if he could take her photo. Rory took advantage of the distraction and slipped away. He'd come to town for a reason. No need to get sidetracked.

Leaving Nikki outside, Rory entered the department store. One of the few he knew to still be in smalltown existence. They'd started their interior Christmas mode a couple weeks ago. Rory walked past all the displays, focusing on the fact he'd come to get a Thanksgiving gift for Sheila. Nothing too big. She wouldn't like him spending too much money on her, especially for Thanksgiving.

Something small but perfect. The problem as he moved from one department to another? He hadn't the slightest idea what that something might be and wandering aimlessly wasn't going to help.

A woman's voice suddenly addressed him. "Are you looking for something special?"

Rory's head jerked in her direction. A young woman with a purple streak in her hair faced him across a counter. "That's exactly what I'm looking for," he said.

"For the lady in your life?"

"For my mother-in-law."

"So, not perfume."

He looked around, noting the bottles arrayed over the counter, and snorted a short laugh. He hadn't meant to pause there. "Not perfume. Something appropriate to Thanksgiving, but special, because, well, she's been there for me through…through a lot."

"Oh, how sweet," the woman gushed. Rory almost walked away then and there, but he held firm.

"Any suggestions?" he asked.

"Does she like flowers?"

"Only in the garden."

"Does she collect anything?"

Rory thought for a minute. "Tea cups," he said.

"Tea cups?"

Rory nodded.

"Ah," said the salesperson. She leaned forward to whisper. "There are some beautiful tea sets over there." She pointed.

Rory followed her pointing finger to a section

displaying fine china. Feeling large and clumsy, he shoved his hands back into his pockets and walked around carefully, eyeing the displays. Finally, he reached out and lifted an extremely delicate-looking cup with a cardinal on it. Like her daughter, Sheila loved cardinals. He turned the cup back and forth several times. After a moment, he put it down.

"Not doing it for you?"

Rory spun toward Tessa's voice. "I'm looking for a gift for Sheila." Even he could hear the defensiveness in his voice.

"For Christmas?"

"For Thanksgiving."

Tessa's brows lowered. "Like a hostess type gift?"

"Is that the only type you give at Thanksgiving?" he asked.

"Usually. Why? What did you have in mind?"

Blowing a breath past his lips, Rory avoided Tessa's eye when he answered. "Something to thank her. To thank them both, really, for sticking by me."

Tessa reached out, touched his arm. "And why wouldn't they stick by you, Rory? You did nothing wrong."

He kept any reply to himself.

"Honestly," Tessa suggested quietly, "why don't you wait until Christmas? I...I know you've not been celebrating, but maybe this is the year to do it, yes? You'll come up with something perfect between now and then."

Rory inhaled, released the air slowly. "You're right." Lightly touching the fingers on his arm, he nodded and walked straight across the store and out through the doors. He spotted Nikki beneath the outdoor lighting, still talking to some folks who'd not yet gone. She turned, almost like she sensed him there, and took a step in his direction. He shook his head at her, raised his hand in a brief wave, and hurried off to his truck.

Driving through the dark to his home, his real home, the home he had shared for so many years with his wife, he considered all the so-called stages of grief. He'd read, heard, been told, learned in a group environment, they didn't happen to everyone in the exact order outlined, or to each individual at all, that it took longer with some than others. He was tired of hearing it. Tired of living it. He desperately wanted the last one: acceptance.

Rory pulled into his driveway, drove slowly along the graveled track. The lights from his truck swept across the housefront. He remembered those nights he'd convinced himself he'd see Kat there still, waiting for him at the door. He remembered those nights he understood he never would.

Alerted to pending precipitation by the local news forecast, he pulled the truck into the garage, sat inside for countless minutes, thinking about so many things. Only when he climbed out did he recall the pie he'd needed to collect from Gina Hart's bakery. As he stood there undecided about a return into town, a slow-moving car pulled into the driveway. He threw up his hand to block the headlight's glare and exited the open garage, wondering who'd gotten lost. No one pulled into his driveway these days. They used to, coming around to check on him, but now they all waited, patiently, hopefully, for an invite that never came.

The car door opened. A figure he couldn't quite see slipped from the interior.

"Rory?"

Rory froze. It was Nikki.

"Gina grabbed me by my car. She gave me your address and asked if I could drop off this pie on my way back to the Jeffersons." She took two steps closer and stopped. "I...I guess I could have just stuck it in my little fridge until tomorrow."

Still, he said nothing. He heard her breath huff out.

"Or I could set it on the ground like people do for wild animals, hoping you'll come and get it once I've gone away."

He pictured himself waiting immobile until Nikki pulled away in her car before scurrying over to the pie, sniffing it for good measure, and then running into the house with it. The image her sarcastic words evoked was so vivid and so ridiculous, he started to laugh.

"I'm sorry," he said. "I...I'm sorry. I didn't mean to be rude."

He pulled down the garage door and started in her direction. She met him halfway, holding the pie out at arm's length. In the headlights from her running car, he saw the crooked twist to her mouth. He couldn't quite tell what she was thinking, but he took the pie from her with a thank you and another apology for his behavior.

"Stop," she said. "I get it. I'll see you tomorrow, yes?"

"Yes," he answered. She backed up, pivoted on her heel, headed back toward her car. "Nikki, wait! Do you—" She turned around, faced him. He took a deep breath, like he was about to plunge headfirst into an icy lake, and forced the next words out. Pushing himself. "Would you like to come in for a few minutes?"

He could tell how shaky he sounded. So, apparently, could Nikki. She smiled at him. A small smile. Not pity. More like understanding.

"Not tonight," she said. "Okay?"

Rory nodded. "Okay."

"I'll see you at dinner." She continued to her car and climbed inside, backed with care along the gravel drive and out onto the road. She flashed the lights once before pulling away. Rory waited until she'd disappeared from sight before he turned, pie in hand, and went inside.

Chapter Fourteen

It had been a long time since Nikki had lost sleep over a man. And that other time hadn't been for good reasons. She wasn't sure this one was either.

Rolling onto her right side, she pounded the pillow with her fist, reshaping it beneath her head. Outside she heard a muted sound like a scream. Not the first time, but tonight it made her jump. A female fox, Sheila had told her when she brought it up before. Nikki had seen a fox the next day, running through the stubbled field across the road. *Home* contained a photo of one, mid-leap in the snow in the very same field. She'd checked, just to be sure, comparing the woods in the distance, the fieldstone house at the far end. Coincidence? Sure. But coincidences seemed to be mounting where she and Rory were concerned.

Beautiful animals, foxes. She'd always

considered them so. Beautiful man, too, Robert Roderick Hollis. A person could sense that, in his art. He wasn't bad to look at either, by any means, even with his constantly half-shaved beard and faintly haunted eyes. Tonight, though—well, technically last night, she realized after checking her phone again for the time—he had looked…different. Beautiful, yes, but like a man struggling. A new and painful struggle, she figured. Maybe even a struggle long overdue. A struggle involving her, somehow.

She didn't want to cause him any pain. Didn't want to be the one to bring him back to the life he'd known, either. It wasn't her job. She hardly knew him. She didn't need the responsibility, especially if some small thing she did caused it to fail. She'd made enough mistakes, endured enough trauma, both personal and in the physical, nearly-everything-I-own is gone variety. So had Rory, losses greater than her own, yet as significant and life-altering. She'd decided almost immediately Connor Falls was the perfect place for her to come to terms with all the blasted changes in her own life. Now, she wasn't so sure.

She rolled to her left, all the way, until she faced the wall. It occurred to her Rory had faced the same wall on sleepless nights. Probably rested his head on this same pillow in this same bed. With a groan, she rolled again, sat up, tossed off the covers and reached for her robe. She shoved her arms in the sleeves and leapt off the mattress, then tied the belt around her middle. Searching along the floor with her bare toes until she found her slippers,

Nikki hastily shoved her feet inside them, tromped downstairs and built up a small fire on the hearth. Once the flames began leaping along the logs, Nikki pulled up the camp chair and sat staring at the bright tongues.

Sammy would be up if Nikki called her now. Her friend had always been a night owl, and fussed until the wee hours before Thanksgiving. Given the three-hour time difference between East and West coasts made it even more likely Sammy would answer the call. But Nikki's phone still lay on the nightstand and she wasn't inclined to get up from the comfy seat and the lovely warmth to retrieve it. Besides, she didn't really want to talk. She couldn't imagine how to explain the way she felt. She didn't quite understand it herself.

After a few minutes, she leaned sideways, stretching her arm toward the small table where Rory's book lay. Managing to get her fingers around the bound end, she pulled it closer until she could grab with the other hand, too. She settled the book into her lap and stared at the cover.

So very striking. So absolutely telling. No one could deny the artistry and the emotion evident on this and every single page. These photographs were the product of a man deeply in love, not only with his wife but with the life they'd created, and with this town and its environs.

Here sat Nikki Sharp, fancying a little emotion for the man who'd laid his heart bare for the world to see. A beautiful, broken man. A man with such vast emotion now sealed up tight inside him, perhaps fighting to keep it there, where it remained safe and whole despite tragedy.

Yes, here sat Nikki Sharp, a bit broken herself, fighting to keep her own emotions at bay and wondering if it might not be too late to claim something drastic like the flu, so she could avoid Thanksgiving dinner with Rory—and his former in-laws—and remain tucked up in bed until New Year's Day.

*   *   *

Having retrieved the quilt from the bed, Nikki had fallen asleep on the floor before the dying fire sometime after four in the morning, waking up disoriented and later than usual to a knock on the door. Still pushing the hair from her eyes, she opened it without thinking to find Sheila Jefferson standing on the other side.

"Oh, goodness, I'm sorry! You're usually such an early riser," the woman said upon glimpsing Nikki's disheveled state.

Nikki hastened to assure her. "It's okay. No need to apologize. I didn't sleep well last night and curled up in front of the fire. Between the heat and the change of place, I slept like a baby after. Which is why," she added, pointing to the doubtlessly creased contours of her face, "I look like this. What's up?"

Sheila appeared embarrassed, her gaze sliding away and back to Nikki's. "Nothing really. I…" Her voice tapered off.

"Come on, Sheila, spill. What do you need help with?"

Sheila raised her arm, revealing a bandaged pointer finger on her right hand. "I did it this morning. Haven't even begun peeling potatoes or turnips, and a neighbor informed me they will be coming after all."

Nikki grabbed her hand, frowning at the blood seeping through the bandage. "Just let me get my clothes on. I'm happy to help. And I'll look at that, too. Does it need stitches?"

"No. Of course not," Sheila said. "I just need to stop using that finger for a little bit. Thank you, Nikki. Thank you so much."

Sheila shuffled off in her always unfastened boots, back toward the house. Nikki shut the door against the chill air and hurried upstairs to dress. She'd come back later for a shower and change of clothes. Startled into alertness by Sheila's arrival, she almost forgot the reason for her nearly sleepless night. Remembering it as she pulled on her socks and shoes, she briefly pictured herself at the table with Rory. Next to him? Across? Perhaps nowhere near him? The latter was probably best.

Yes, definitely best. Even better if she helped Sheila and then skipped town.

With a rueful laugh, she tugged on her coat, not bothering to button it, and headed out to the large house a brisk, short walk away.

As it ended up, Rory called Sheila and begged off. Nikki knew it was him on the phone when Sheila used his name. Understood the call's nature in Sheila's subtly changing expression from smiling to simply not.

Setting down her cell phone, Sheila blew a

breath past her lips.

"Everything okay?" Nikki asked, giving the potatoes a second rinse before dumping them in the huge pot beside the sink.

Shiela shrugged a shoulder. "Not okay, really, but not unexpected."

Nikki went back to the potatoes. "Rory's not coming?"

"No. And I really thought he might."

Nikki knew there had been something weird in last night's brief exchange between herself and Rory. It had affected her and likely had done the same to him. At least now Nikki didn't have to worry about any accidental, peripheral glances at dinner, or small talk, or worse, making Rory laugh again. His joy always seemed followed by pain. Sheila, though, looked more upset than her casual dismissal let on.

"I didn't mean to eavesdrop," Nikki said, "but I did hear you leave it open-ended. Maybe he'll change his mind and come."

Sheila merely shook her head, looking around the homey kitchen as if she'd lost something. As she had. Two somethings, Nikki realized. Her daughter and—at family times like these anyway— the man she viewed as a son.

"Turnips next?" Nikki asked, hoping to recall Sheila from her sad reverie. Sheila jerked her head with a start.

"Yes," she said. "And thank you again for your help. I should be fine after this. Pete will be back and he'll pitch in. He's good like that."

Nikki set aside the colander she'd been using to

rinse the potatoes. "Not a problem. I'm happy to lend a hand."

A short time later the lesser mass of turnips had been readied for the pot. Nikki glanced about for another job needing doing. The turkey was already prepared for the oven. Apparently, that undertaking had taken place before the nasty cut. "What else can I do?"

"Like I said, Pete will be back soon. I think I can let you get back to your day."

With a snort, Nikki shook her head. "I didn't have anything planned except coming here. Would you like to get the table set? That would be one less thing for later."

Sheila hesitated. Nikki wondered why. Perhaps this was something she liked to do herself. A second later, though, Nikki understood.

"Kat used to do that with me."

Nikki raised her hands. "I'm sorry. I didn't mean to overstep—"

"Oh, no. It's all right. When you asked, it occurred to me how nice it would be to do it with someone again. Pete offers, of course, but really, he's almost literally like a bull in a china shop when it comes to handling dishes and glassware. The crystal quakes at the sight of him."

Nikki had to laugh. She couldn't help it. Sheila possessed such a warm and funny personality. Her daughter probably had, as well. Which gave Rory even more reason to miss her.

Following Sheila into the dining room, Nikki stopped short. Gracing the wall above the buffet hung a large, framed photograph. A family portrait.

Not the kind Nikki was used to, where people posed together in their best clothes, smiles plastered on their faces. No, she saw a wonderful, spontaneous, joyful photo taken right here in this room. It appeared someone had just made a joke, or perhaps they were all in stitches over Rory's antics to get himself into the timed picture. He'd barely made it, caught in mid-hop to a place behind Kat's chair, Sheila and Pete leaning in from either side. The grins were genuine, Kat's eyes nearly shut in long-lashed quarter-moons, the glass in her hand slopping something pale in an arc through the air.

"Oh," Nikki sighed, "I love that."

At the same time, she thought how much it must hurt to see it. Then again, Shiela and Pete had the photo hanging for all to view. Perhaps the reminder of that moment made them happy. Very likely, it made Rory sad. Nikki took a deep breath and turned to face Sheila, steeling herself for whatever expression she might find.

"I love it, too," said Sheila with a broad smile. "I almost peed my pants."

Nikki laughed even harder than she had about the quaking crystal, wishing, actually wishing, Rory could be there to share the laughter. He needed to be part of it.

After the cloth-covered table had been set with what appeared a very old but beautiful china set with a fall motif, along with everything else required for a full dinner, Nikki checked Sheila's hand once more before heading back over to the cottage to shower and catch a quick, much-needed nap. The moment she'd shut the door, however, she pulled out her cell and texted Rory.

If you're not coming because of me, I don't have to go to dinner, but your in-laws need you there. They really do. Am I laying a guilt trip on you? Possibly. Sometimes that's a trip you need to take.

Without waiting for a reply, she dropped the phone on the counter, hustled up the stairs, gathered fresh clothes, and headed into the bathroom to shower.

Chapter Fifteen

Rory stared down at his cell phone, his jaw clenched. How dare she? She was nothing in his life and yet she thought she could take him to task like a scolding mother. And about this, of all things.

His jaw muscles released and he expelled a long, slow breath, watching the frosty cloud drift away. Sheila had let him off the hook too easily. He'd let himself off the hook with the same ease. Yet, it wasn't her place to fight him back to life. Nor was it Nikki's. It was his own responsibility to do so. Last night—was it only last night? Yes, last night he'd told himself the time had come. Sometime during those sleepless hours, he'd decided otherwise.

Muttering a few, unkind words at himself, he slipped his cell phone back into his pocket with one hand and zipped his jacket all the way to his chin with the other. The weather had changed. Gotten colder. More brittle with only a damp hint caressing his skin. He recognized everything about the change. Snow was on its way.

I'll do it if it snows.

He'd lied.

But here he was, trudging through the stubbled fields with a camera slung around his neck. He'd had to clean the dust from the strap, it had been so long. The case, too. Once upon a time, he went nowhere without at least one of his cameras. Kat had joked about his "obsession." She'd claimed that if not for her, the only thing he'd remember to bring on a trip would be his camera equipment. That he might, when pushed, forget even her.

His mouth twisted at the memory. Two parts amusement, and only one part regret. Moving forward. Getting better.

Rory cut across the open area toward an abandoned building on the property. A small structure, constructed from fieldstone. He'd spotted Charlie Williams earlier and asked if it would be okay to walk in the fields. Charlie had been quite surprised to see him, Rory could tell, but had merely given him a nod in permission and continued into his barn. He'd never been much for conversation, old Charlie. That was fine. Rory didn't feel in the mood for small talk anyway.

The harvested remains from corn stalks caught at Rory's boot laces. Several times he had to lift his foot and shake himself free. Mice rustled away from his approach, one with an old corn kernel in its mouth, no doubt taking the food to its nest. Rory spotted a fox in the distance, and a minute later several deer bounded away from the forest edge where they'd been standing, blended into the background. The tension in his back and shoulders loosened as he walked. He began to view Nikki's text with less annoyance. Although she'd only been in Connor Falls less than a week, she appeared to care a great deal about the people she'd met. He knew he'd disappointed Sheila and Pete. Maybe he'd disappointed Nikki, as well, but he didn't really want to think about that.

Yeah, fat chance not thinking about it now.

The light at this point was perfect. He pushed everything else from his mind and strode up to the building, eyeing the stones for texture, gradient, striations, shadow. A small maple grew right inside an unglazed window. Several brilliant orange leaves clung to the narrow branch poking out toward the world. Rory decided to start there, his heart not yet invested, but soon he was framing and photographing images with a renewed and remembered spark. He kept going until the light changed. Glancing around, he saw the sun trying to break through the pale grey clouds. It still felt like snow, though. When it began, would Nikki recall his promise?

Probably. It seemed like something she would remember.

And Sheila? He'd made her a promise, too. A

promise he'd be there for Thanksgiving dinner this year.

Pulling out his phone, he glanced at the hour. A long sigh escaped him.

There was still time. Still time to go home, shower, and show up with his bakery pie.

Sighing again, he slipped his phone back into his pocket and returned to taking photographs despite the altered light.

*   *   *

While Nikki dressed with care for dinner, she couldn't help the niggling, ridiculous notion she was somehow stepping in as a placeholder for Sheila and Pete's daughter. A placeholder for a woman who wouldn't return. However, if it gave them extra solace on this family day, so be it. She was happy to bring them comfort. Or just be company, plain and simple. The neighbors' attendance would help, too. This would be a bright, enjoyable day for all. Including Nikki. She wanted to gather with them as much as they wanted her there.

Rory needed it more, though. Nikki had half a mind to get in her car and drive over to his place, drag him out kicking and screaming, if necessary. But she wouldn't. It would serve no purpose. He had to come on his own. Even so, she couldn't help a short fantasy playing in her mind in which she threw open Rory's front door, barged into his home, grabbed his shirtfront and marched him over to his in-laws.

"Not my job," she muttered under her breath as she opened her own door and stepped outside. A car was parked near her own by the barn. The neighbors, she presumed. On the vehicle's opposite side, she spotted the familiar profile of Rory's pickup truck. And beside it, just climbing out, Rory himself.

She hadn't seen him in anything besides work clothes since that evening three years ago. Right then, beneath a nicely-cut, black, wool coat he wore a sage-green tie, an actual tie, lying against a shirt bearing the most exquisite plum color. Nikki glanced down at the simple, long-sleeved, sage green dress she'd put on. She couldn't have picked a better complement to his attire if they'd set out to coordinate it. She'd have to change into something else. She would just have to. Before she could step back inside the cottage, Rory spotted her and called her name.

Taking a deep breath, she pulled the door shut behind her and strode in his direction. Nearly at his side, she paused.

"I got the note you passed me in class," she said.

He looked confused.

With a crooked smile, she pointed from her dress to his tie.

He glanced down, then back up at her. "Ah. Got it."

"And the pie?"

He jumped with a small exclamation and

hurried back to the truck to retrieve the box, returning a second later. "Your cookies?"

"I brought them over earlier," Nikki said.

They both stood awkwardly on the walkway, Nikki suppressing a shiver in the absence of her coat.

"Look, I—" Rory started.

"Sheila and Pete will be so happy you're here," Nikki interrupted whatever Rory had been about to say. "I'm glad you changed your mind."

"Your text wasn't a guilt trip. It was a reminder I needed," he said. "I almost stayed home anyway, but I...well, I..."

"Changed your mind. No decision is ever permanent until after its execution. And not even then." Nikki shrugged. "Stuff happens."

"Stuff happens," he murmured in agreement.

Nikki jerked her head toward the Jeffersons' front door. "Let's get inside. I'm freezing. And if it comes up, we didn't know what the other was wearing. Got it?"

Rory hastened after her. "We didn't," he said.

Nikki laughed. "I know that. But it's a peculiar coincidence, you've got to admit."

Not for the first time, Nikki realized coincidences thrived where she and Rory were concerned.

*   *   *

Rory took a seat at the dining table with the framed photograph behind him. He loved the photo for so many reasons, but didn't want to look at it right now for so many more. Nikki sat diagonally across from him with Bill Tudor's wife at her side. Bill himself sat to Rory's left, Pete and Sheila at each end. At Nikki and Rose's backs a few logs burned in the fireplace. Not a huge fire. Enough to make the room comfortably toasty, though. The table itself was laden with food they'd all carried in. No one stood on ceremony here.

Pete made his usual speech about gratitude, thankfulness for all they had, and for the time spent with friends and family. Even absent family. Rory felt the hair on his arms lift beneath his sleeves, almost as if a ghost had entered the room. His gaze slid from side to side, taking in the expressions on his former in-laws faces. They were smiling at each other as if no one else in the room existed. Private smiles. Sad smiles. Hopeful smiles. Wistful smiles. Rory's chest tightened.

"And to friends old and new," Pete finished up, raising his glass of homemade mead. Everyone else followed suit, lifting glasses and making the appropriate sounds. Rory's eyes shifted to Nikki and away when he found her gaze meeting his.

Throughout dinner, everyone behaved as if Rory had never removed himself from the traditional gathering. Never spent the holidays away from them. The only acknowledgment came when Sheila reached her hand over to his quite unobtrusively, and squeezed it on the tabletop.

After dinner, Sheila as usual refused all offers to help with cleanup besides refrigerating leftovers and piling dishes in a sink filled with warm water.

"You know me," Sheila said. "Dishes can wait. Company shouldn't."

As late afternoon progressed into evening, and they all moved into the living room and a homey fire on another hearth, Rory relaxed, joined in the conversation, even laughed at Sheila's retelling the portrait story to the Tudors. They'd probably heard the brief tale before, but they didn't seem to mind.

"You're a very talented photographer, Rory," Rose said to him. "I have your book on my coffee table. When are we going to see something else from you?"

The abrupt silence was broken by an intake of breath. Whose, Rory couldn't tell. He straightened his shoulders despite the weight he suddenly felt on them. "Actually," he said, "I was out today for a bit with my camera. The first time since…since before Kat passed."

The words didn't break him. In fact, they hurt no more than a swift, nearly bloodless cut. Sheila walked up behind him where he sat near the fire and put her arms around him, leaning her chin on his head. He patted her hand a little awkwardly. From the corner of his eye, he spotted Nikki looking away from them, her suspiciously moist eyes reflecting the firelight.

Sheila straightened, releasing him. "Anybody

for dessert? Rory brought a scrumptious pumpkin pie and Nikki got us some of Gina's wonderful gingerbread cookies."

Dessert and coffee were eaten in the living room in the fire's vicinity. The grandfather clock chimed the hour as Pete stood to ask who wanted seconds. Rory startled. He stood also.

"I'm sorry, I'm going to have to leave," he said.

"Are you all right?" asked Sheila.

"Yes," said Rory, starting toward the kitchen with his plate. He stopped, spun on his heel. "I— when I changed my mind about coming to dinner, I decided I should make an all-out effort and told my brother I'd stop over there, too." He looked ruefully at the pumpkin-smeared plate in his hand. "For dessert," he added.

Sheila's gentle smile broadened into a grin. She threw her arms around him again. "I'm so happy you were here this year. Thank you."

"No," said Rory soberly, "thank you."

Nikki rose from her chair. "May I package up a few of the cookies I brought for Rory to take with him? I think Lyddie would like them."

"Lyddie loves gingerbread," Rory said, turning to her. "She has very grown-up taste."

Nikki moved her head in agreement. "She's a very grown-up little girl."

Sheila observed the exchange between them, an amused smile fluttering on her face. "I have a couple of small brown paper bags. Let's fill one, shall we?"

Rory said goodnight to everyone and followed Sheila into the kitchen, where he retrieved his coat from the wall rack and shoved his arms into the sleeves. Sheila located the bags, fitted one with wax paper inside, then handed it to Nikki, still with the same, slightly entertained smile. She patted Rory once on the arm before striding from the room.

"There are a lot of cookies left in here," Nikki said without looking at him. "How many should I send over, do you think? Seven?"

"Seven works," Rory answered, studying her profile. She seemed to be giving all her attention to the way she put the cookies inside the bag. "Are you okay?"

She nodded, glanced his way, then turned back to her task. "Are you?"

"Yeah," he said, after a moment. "Right now, I definitely am."

"Good." Pivoting, Nikki grabbed Rory's hand and plopped the bag onto his open palm. "Tell Luke and Lyddie I said hi and happy Thanksgiving, will you?"

There seemed something personal in the request, something indicative of familiarity, comfort, friendship. "Of course," he said. "Happy Thanksgiving, Nikki. Thanks for not letting me off the hook."

She shrugged and pushed him lightly toward the door. He reached for the knob, looked back at her.

"You could come with me if you like," he

said. "Would you like?"

"I would," Nikki said softly, "which is precisely why I won't. It's your family time. Make the most it, Rory. I'll see you tomorrow, I guess? Or did you take the day off?"

Rory opened the door and stepped outside, drawing a deep breath. "I haven't decided yet," he said over his shoulder. "But…"

"But?" Nikki prompted.

"It smells like snow out here, so you might see me either way."

Chapter Sixteen

Nikki watched Rory through the curtain, eyeing his long stride all the way to his truck. Before he might turn around and discover her spying on him, she let the curtain drop and stepped away from the door.

Rory Hollis hadn't forgotten his promise.

She wasn't quite sure what crazy machinations his remembering performed on rational thought, but her heart felt strangely mobile, like it might be dancing. Foolish, but oddly welcome. She possessed an urge to skip back into the living room. Good thing she didn't, because when she spun around, she found Sheila had returned to the kitchen. Arching her eyebrows, Nikki jerked a thumb over her shoulder.

"He's off," she said. "That's good, right?"

"Very good," agreed Sheila. "We're thinking about playing a board game. Do you want to join in?"

"Sure. What are we playing?"

"Clue," Sheila said.

"Wow, I haven't played that in forever. Sounds good." She trailed at Sheila's back, picturing them all figuring out who did in whom with what and in which room for the rest of the evening. That, another gingerbread cookie, and more of Pete's mead would make the night perfect.

By the time Nikki headed to the cottage, the hands on the grandfather clock in the Jeffersons' living room had moved well past midnight. She was feeling mildly tipsy from the mead and little sleep. It took a few moments for her to realize the light touch on her face and hands came from icy precipitation. Snowflakes, quite tiny and sporadic, but snow all the same. Rory and his sensitive nose had been right.

Inside, Nikki retrieved her coat and put it on. She kicked off her shoes, not caring where they landed, and pulled on her fleece-lined boots. Tucking a knit cap on her head, she scurried back outside to stand beneath the midnight sky, face up, enjoying the flakes skipping across her skin. An owl hooted, a low sound like two repeated sentences. From what Nikki knew about owls and how far their voices traveled, the bird could have been a couple miles away or in the woods across the road. A few seconds later she heard an answering call, seeming to come from the huge tree in the Jeffersons' front yard. Try as she might, she couldn't see the creature. She took a few steps closer to the oak. The front door to the house opened. Sheila and her two neighbors exited, stopping short upon seeing Nikki.

"Sorry," Nikki apologized. She pointed upward. "There's an owl in your tree and I was trying to see it."

"Wait right there," Sheila said, "and I'll show you."

She walked Bill and Rose to their car, wished them a good-night and a happy Thanksgiving. They waved to Pete in the doorway before getting in their car. Pete shut the front door. Sheila watched the car leave the driveway. With a small sound, she turned and strode in Nikki's direction.

"Come this way," she said, curling her fingers. Nikki followed her around the tree to a place where a huge branch had broken off, years ago by the weathered edges, leaving a hollow over time. "Up there. You might not see him now, but in the summer, I sit very quietly at night and wait for him to come out to hunt. It's a bit cold for us to do that tonight. Oh, look, did you see the movement?"

Nikki wasn't sure, although she thought she might have. "What type is it?"

"A barred owl. They're pretty big. Do you like birds of prey?"

"I like nature in general," Nikki answered. "I'm a bit of a sucker for moments like these."

Sheila's lips curved. "You should look through Rory's book again, then. He has a photo of this very owl, flying up into the tree with a mouse it caught."

Nikki's breath circled like smoke. "I'll check that out. I could tell by what I did see in his book that Rory loved this area and your daughter. His life."

"He still does," Sheila whispered.

"I didn't mean—"

Lifting her fingers, Sheila stopped her words. "I know," she whispered. "What I'm saying is, he needs to recognize it again. Come to terms with his losses and embrace what he still has."

Nikki remained quiet.

"They were very different from each other, Rory and Katrina," Sheila went on, softer now. She might have been talking to herself if not for her gaze shifting toward Nikki and away again. That little shift prompted Nikki to ask questions.

"In what way?"

"Kat had grand ideas. Plans she hoped would take her away from our little town. She wasn't a nature lover. Not like you. Not like me. Not like Rory. Smalltown life wasn't for her either, even though she'd been born and raised in Connor Falls. I encouraged her to fly, though. To spread her wings and follow her dreams. It's every child's right, you know?"

Nikki's parents had encouraged her, too, when they were alive. But not all parents were like that, Nikki knew. "So, what happened? She met Rory?"

Sheila nodded. "Yes. She met Rory. Love changed everything. For them both, I think. Sometimes it was rough, setting new goals, or seeking to accomplish the same ones through a different perspective. But they made it work. And then Kat got sick. Everything changed again, for all of us."

Nikki reached out, slipped her hand into Sheila's. Sheila's hand jerked, but she didn't pull away. Her fingers tightened around Nikki's in return.

"I'm so sorry for your loss," Nikki whispered.

"Thank you, Nikki," Sheila said. "It's not fresh, but in moments like these it feels as though it is. And yet, talking about her makes me feel better. I just wish Rory would do more of that and not keep it bottled up inside. With me, or someone else. Not with you."

Nikki glanced at the woman sidelong. Sheila's gaze remained on the tree. "Why not?" Nikki asked, shaken by the remark.

"Because he seems to like you, and he shouldn't unburden himself by making the burden yours. It wouldn't be fair to you."

"I don't know what to say, Sheila. I like him, too, and as a friend I'm willing to listen when he needs to talk. There's nothing wrong with that."

"No," agreed Sheila on a sigh. "There's nothing wrong with that."

She seemed to want to say something more, but at that moment the front door opened. Pete stuck his head out.

"What're you two ladies doing out there?"

Shiela dropped Nikki's hand. "Watching the owl."

"You can see it?"

"Not really," said Nikki, taking a step toward the cottage.

"I've a hankering for a turkey sandwich. Anyone else?"

Patting her stomach, Nikki shook her head. "I'm full, Pete, but thanks. Thanks to you both for a great night." She turned to Sheila. "If you leave the dishes in the sink, I'll pop over in the morning to lend a hand with them."

"Sure," said Sheila. "That would be great. I'll make some mashed potato omelets for breakfast."

"Yum," Nikki answered with a somewhat forced grin. Her conversation with Sheila had troubled her. Waving to the couple, Nikki crossed the lawn and went inside. The last thing she saw before closing the door was Sheila heading inside with her husband.

That, and the fact the snow had stopped.

Chapter Seventeen

Despite the late hour, Nikki broke out *Home* again, looking through the pages for the photo Sheila had mentioned. She found it, the graceful, barred owl like a shadow in the night, the details of its body highlighted by the moon, or perhaps the solar lamp burning in the yard. She could just make out the mouse dangling in its short, curved beak. Although Nikki thought mice adorable, she considered the owl's meal with a pragmatic eye. After spending several long minutes examining the haunting picture and the caption beneath, she slowly closed the book, studying once more Rory's wife on the cover.

Strange, what Sheila had said about Rory not making his grief Nikki's burden. Was she seeing something Nikki couldn't? Or maybe it had been a gentle warning not to be brought down by it. So far, though, she hadn't been. She understood. Someone's understanding without dismissal or getting too wrapped up in the emotions was a good thing, wasn't it? Even though Nikki didn't know Rory very well, she considered herself a friend. Sometimes, in strange, quiet moments, more than a friend. Perhaps, this was the purpose behind Sheila's words.

Nikki picked up the book and stood, sliding the volume back onto the table. Enough. Time to get some real sleep. She'd promised Sheila she'd be over in the morning to help with the dishes. Which meant early. No sleeping in.

She woke with the sun, wanting nothing more than to turn over and go back to dreaming. Instead, Nikki pushed the covers off and started her day. Before getting dressed, she checked her emails, answered one from Sammy and one from an acquaintance back in Brewster, and found little else but nonsense. It was only the day after Thanksgiving after all. A bit soon to get responses for the new year's window work. Most jobs would be back in Brewster, she knew. Whether she wanted to or not, she'd have to return there, find a new place to live, settle in again. Right now, though, in this quiet place, a return held no appeal.

Fine. She accepted that. She'd come to Connor Falls with a plan to heal from recent events. Center herself again. Her current schedule gave her about five weeks to do so. Nikki shut down her laptop, reminding herself that whenever notice came in, she sometimes did her best work when rushed. Hannah's was a perfect example.

Except Nikki's life wasn't confined to the work cycle. Work was only a part of life, a concept she'd tried in recent years to regrasp. Well, with upheaval came change.

"Right," she grumbled to herself sarcastically. "No hurry then."

Dressing in warm leggings and an oversized comfy sweatshirt, Nikki once again pulled on her boots and then picked up her phone, sending Sheila a text. She didn't want to just march over there. Considering the time they'd all gone to bed, Sheila might have opted for extra sleep over dishes first thing. While waiting for a response, Nikki peeked through the side curtain toward the barn. She saw Rory's truck conspicuously absent and glanced at the battery-powered wall clock, double-checking the time. Maybe he wasn't coming to work today. She couldn't blame him. After going over to his brother's, he'd probably had a late night, too. Whatever the reason, it was no business of hers.

Ten minutes later, she decided Sheila must be sleeping in and put on her coat, determined to take a walk, get some fresh air in her lungs, oxygen in her brain. Outside, she pulled the knit hat on, and walked down the driveway to the road.

She rarely saw traffic on this section of rural blacktop. No shoulders existed, but she'd have notice enough to step off onto the verge if a car came along. Tucking gloveless hands into her pockets, she turned left, the way she came to the

Jeffersons from town. No reason for it except familiarity and the fact the light wind blew at her back.

Walking always helped clear Nikki's mind. Even as a kid, if something upset her or she faced a difficult issue, she'd head out for a long walk. The rigorous monotony, soles crunching repeatedly on pavement, her respiration's eventual deep rhythm, served to settle her thoughts and let them recede to the background.

She had decisions to make and despite the old saying, 'never put off until tomorrow,' she was going to do exactly that. It wouldn't do her any good to make those decisions while she still felt turmoil regarding what she'd left behind. She needed to work through those things first and then make up her mind. So, she kept walking, leaving the Jeffersons' acreage far behind and checking every so often to see if Sheila had texted back. A vast squawking and honking slowly grew louder, until Nikki spotted more Canada geese than she could count gathered in the field across the road. She crossed over to watch them, keeping her distance. Geese, she knew firsthand, could get cranky and aggressive if disturbed.

In an enclosed area, the sound from the fowl would have been cacophonous, but here in the open it seemed a counterpoint to the wind and other small noises, flowing together like water. Folding her arms across her chest, Nikki allowed herself to sink into the sound, ignoring the chill as her body cooled down from the walk. The geese shifted positions in a subtle manner, occasionally winging into the air to land again somewhere nearby. It was like a dance, really. Nikki wondered if Rory had ever tried to capture it through his camera's lens. Rory, with his romantic, magical eye.

Yes. Rory.

Thoughts turning to Rory, her calm seeped away to be replaced by speculation, a small thrill, and concern. A mix of emotions that ended her walk. Turning on her heel, she headed back the way she'd come. Halfway to the house, a vehicle approached in the far lane behind her and slowed to match her pace. She stepped well off the road and took up a defensive stance, her face deliberately marked by attitude. She didn't care if this was Connor Falls. Never trust a stranger who thinks it's okay to address someone on a lonely stretch of tarmac.

The driver's side window rolled down on a familiar pickup truck.

"Rory!"

"Sorry," he said. "Did I scare you?"

"Maybe a little."

"Sorry," he apologized again. "Are you going back to the house? Want a lift?"

He sounded perfectly normal. At ease. In the meantime, her heart raced in a cardiac dance not entirely due to the fact she'd momentarily pictured him as a malevolent stranger. Simply put, Rory made her heart beat faster. Corny, perhaps a little melodramatic, but true. Blowing out a long breath, Nikki nodded and crossed the road to his truck, where she climbed into the passenger's side. After she hooked her seatbelt, she folded her hands in her lap.

"How was the rest of your evening?" Nikki asked, her eyes on the road ahead.

"Fun," Rory answered. "I shouldn't be avoiding all of this. Still, if I'm honest, staying focused on the present wore me out. But I recognize it's good for me."

Nikki glanced his way. "So, one step forward, no steps back?"

His lips turned up. "So far."

Nikki wanted to reach across and squeeze his arm, the way Sheila might have. Unlike Sheila, though, there would have been nothing maternal in the touch. Nikki kept her hands still, watching Rory from the corner of her eye. Rory flicked on the turn signal and she realized they had reached the Jeffersons' driveway. As they pulled in, Nikki spotted Sheila knocking at the cottage door. Sheila turned at the truck's tires crunching over gravel. Her eyes widened when she saw Nikki climbing from the passenger side the instant the pickup came to a complete stop in its usual parking space. At the woman's expression, heat crawled up Nikki's throat into her face. A stupid reaction. A guilty one, for no better reason than Nikki liked the man who had once been this woman's son-in-law. Still was, as far as Sheila was concerned.

Pulling herself together, Nikki hurried to

Sheila's side, yanking her phone from her pocket to see if she'd ending up missing Sheila's text after all. Nope.

"Are you okay?" Sheila asked, cocking her head to one side.

"Cold," Nikki answered. "Lucky for me Rory came along, or I'd still be walking."

"Oh! You went for a walk?" Sheila's gaze slid from Nikki to Rory and back again.

Nikki decided not to explain herself. She worried Sheila thought she had been with Rory somehow, but it was a ridiculous notion—and perhaps a paranoid one on Nikki's part—not worth fussing about. Instead, she said, "I saw a huge flock of Canada geese in one of the fields. I don't think I've ever seen so many in one place. It was pretty amazing. Are we ready for dishes?"

Sheila stared at her a moment too long, and then her lips curved. "Breakfast, first. Rory, breakfast? Mashed potato omelets."

Nikki glanced back to find Rory had exited the truck. "I'd love one. Thanks, Sheila. Just let me lug a couple things inside. I'll lend a hand in the kitchen once I've brought them in. Manning the toaster."

Sheila started a little at his last statement. Her eyes shone briefly before she blinked the tear-sheen away. Nikki wondered if "manning the toaster" had been a regular thing at one point, perhaps when the four of them breakfasted as a family. Rory looked equally taken aback by what he'd said. He hurried to the truck bed and began removing items from inside.

"Want any help carrying stuff in?" Nikki offered.

Rory shook his head without looking up. "I'm good. Thanks."

Yeah, Nikki thought, he had been. One step forward, and maybe just a half step back.

Chapter Eighteen

Rory lifted his head at the thud from a vehicle door closing. He'd set up his table saw outside to keep the mess down in the house. From where he stood working in the chill afternoon, he had a clear view between the trees to the driveway and saw Nikki backing her car from her space by the barn. He wondered for a moment where she might be going and quickly dismissed the question from his mind, returning to the task at hand.

He was nearly finished with his in-laws' house. He had several other jobs lined up through the holidays. He loved carpentry work, any woodworking, really, almost as much as he'd loved his photographic pursuits. The other tasks that occasionally went along with what was termed 'handyman' work, like painting ceilings, walls, and trim, were merely necessary to making a living. He enjoyed wood best. The smell of it, the natural textures, the way it took stain, transforming its beauty to something even deeper. He'd made quite a few furniture items in the past, some of which he'd sold for handsome prices. Except for the tools he utilized for home remodeling and repair now, his woodshop remained idle. He'd covered up a long time ago the areas he didn't use, the projects half-finished. When he walked into his shop these days, all the canvas tarps made it appear like an empty home filled with ghosts.

Rory shut off the saw, clutched the precisely cut trim in his hand, and released a long, slow breath. Everywhere he went felt empty. It wasn't the places. It was him.

Sheila was waiting in the room when he returned inside. As he opened the door, he heard her voice calling out to Pete, who'd come home around noon, leaving the store in his employees' hands. As Pete liked pointing out every year, only certain people did their Black Friday Christmas shopping in a hardware store.

Sheila spun at Rory's approach. "I was just at your brother's ordering a tree. Frank had to leave early for some reason and he's swamped. Those youngsters he has filling in aren't quite sure what they're doing. Why don't you shut down here? There's plenty of time to finish. You could give Luke a hand."

Avoiding Sheila's eye, Rory bent and placed the trim on a tarp on the floor. Once he'd sized them all to make sure they fit properly, he had to stain them. When he straightened, he crossed his arms over his chest.

"You don't need to orchestrate my life, Sheila,"

he said quietly. "I'll survive. I'll get better. I already am."

He could see in her eyes the urge to shake him, to say 'not quickly enough,' but she remained silent. Her lips twisted to one side, her brows attempting to meet above the bridge of her nose. Kat had possessed the same expression when exasperated with him. Like mother, like daughter.

"But I'll go," he said. "I know how crazy it is over there today. I'll just bring the saw and the extension cord in first."

Sheila's expression smoothed out, then crinkled in a smile. "I love you, Rory. We all do. You know that, right?"

"I do. And I love you, too. You've never been anything but wonderful to me. I love you for who you are. Pete, too. And for the daughter you raised. She represented the best of you both."

Sheila swiped at her eyes with her knuckles. "Darn it, Rory, that's twice in two days. Stop making me cry."

"Not meaning to," he answered with a watery smile. "We've all done enough of that."

Wiping her damp hands on her sweatshirt, she met his gaze and held it. He knew what was coming. "It's time for you to move forward, Rory."

"I know that," he said. "I do know that."

They stared at each other for a drawn-out moment. Pete's voice echoed through the house. Sheila turned her head, but not her eyes. "Coming!" she called, before returning her full attention to Rory. "Do something fun. Something out of character. Okay?"

"Sure," Rory responded, not at all sure what that something might be. "I'll try."

He went to retrieve his saw after that, and Sheila to find out why Pete had called her name. Within ten minutes, Rory had backed his truck out and found himself heading for his brother's tree farm.

*　　*　　*

Rory parked at a distance from the barn so as not to interfere with customers. Knowing how cold it would get working outside for an extended period, he jerked on his coat as he strode across the dirt and gravel lot. People were everywhere. He recognized some, but not nearly all. Connor Falls residents and many from beyond. Luke did a booming business with the tree farm their dad had turned over to him. Wreaths, decorated and plain, hung on the barn's exterior walls. He didn't know who helped with decorating them, although likely still their mom, maybe with Lyddie's help. The wreaths were and had always been executed with nature in mind, adorned by other greens, pinecones, dried flowers, twigs, holly cuttings, whatever weeds grew and could be dried into enhancing attachments.

Rory marched past them into the barn, walking straight up to his brother's back as he pushed a cut tree through the machine that bound them. A balsam fir, from the smell, the needle color, the configuration. Rory had learned well those summers he and Luke helped with the planting, the pruning and care, and during the seasonal havoc.

Sensing someone behind him, Luke glanced back. "Rory! What are you doing here?"

"My duty, according to Sheila," Rory answered, smiling. "She said Frank had to leave."

"Yup, yup, he did. Something to do with one of his kids." Luke thanked the customer, handed the tree to a nearby teen with directions to follow the man out to his car, and readied to take the next.

Rory eyed the customers waiting in line. "Where do you want me?"

"Right here would be good. I need to head into the fields. Those boys out there really don't know their trees from their—"

"Got it," said Rory, his smile widening. He took his brother's place and passed the next customer's tree first onto the shaker and then backwards through what was basically a barrel which enclosed the evergreen in netted string to draw the branches together for the ride home. Those customers who knew him greeted Rory warmly. If they felt any surprise finding him there, they made no mention. One by one the line reduced. The Friday after Thanksgiving—especially a late in the month Thanksgiving—was a traditional tree-buying day for many.

Finally, a break came. A teenaged girl hired for the day and wearing a Luke's Tree Farm sweatshirt made her way into the barn lugging a small tree with a wrapped root ball. No one else was in sight. Rory knew there would be another queue soon. He'd done this enough in the past.

Taking the tree from the girl, Rory glanced

around the barn behind her. "Where's the customer?" he asked. Until they arrived, he wasn't inclined to wrap the tree. Sometimes, although not often, people had special instructions.

"Outside," the girl answered. "Looking at wreaths."

Rory leaned the tree against a table and grabbed a broom to sweep the evergreen needles off the floor while he waited. Hearing footsteps, he dumped the dustpan's contents into the bin and turned.

"Rory? Hi."

For a full two seconds, Rory stared at Nikki, a knit hat askew on her head and her cheeks pink from the cold. She held a wreath in her hand.

"I—is this tree yours?" he asked, pointing at the evergreen in question.

"Yes. I just wanted something small for the cottage."

He nodded, feeling suddenly awkward. He picked up the tree and deposited it on the shaker. "So," he said, his back to her, "you're a Friday after Thanksgiving tree person?"

"Not usually, but this year…yeah."

He relinquished his hold on the switch without turning the machine on and pivoted to face her. "Because of everything that happened this year?"

"That, and the fact nearly everyone in this town seems so into Christmas."

She smiled at him, almost apologetically. Maybe because she figured he wasn't into it, at all. He wouldn't deny the truth in her assumption if she mentioned it, but she didn't. Instead, she flopped the wreath onto the counter, fluffed the bow on it.

"What are you doing here?" she asked. "Helping out your brother, I guess? It is very busy." She looked over her shoulder. "Or was. There are a lot of people outside, so I expect they'll be in soon."

"Frank—his right-hand man—had to leave. Family matter, I think." He turned on the shaker, momentarily drowning out any attempts at conversation. After the machine had done its job, Rory ran the tree through the bailer. He then rang up Nikki's purchases on the register. She paid in cash and he handed her the change. "Did Sheila know you were coming here?"

Nikki frowned, thinking. "I don't think so. Why? Does she need something picked up from here? I'd be happy—"

"No. I was just curious."

Nikki gave him a quizzical look.

"It's nothing," Rory said. He wasn't about to explain to her the brief suspicion flashing through his mind, that Sheila had sent him here because she knew Nikki would be at Luke's as well. Matchmaking didn't seem likely. Especially considering she was, or had been, his mother-in-law. Sure, she wanted to see him happy, but—

Did she really think Nikki could bring him back into the world? It wasn't up to Nikki to wrestle him from his lingering grief. Nor Sheila. He had to do it himself.

"Rory?"

He looked up from the receipt he'd been holding absently in his hand. Abruptly, he handed the paper to her. "I don't remember which state it is, but one of them had a law—maybe still does—that you couldn't transport a cut tree without the receipt."

With one arching brow, Nikki turned the slip over in her hand before returning her attention to him. Her mouth twisted in amusement. "Not here though?"

"No. Sorry, I'm rambling."

Catching her lip in her teeth, she studied him a moment. "Well, then," she said, releasing it, "I'll get out of your way. They're lining up again."

She grabbed the wreath in one hand and slipped her other through the knotted material around the tree, walking away before he could call someone to assist her. With the root ball, it couldn't exactly be light, but she didn't appear to need help, anyway.

"You look a little lost, Rory," said the next person in line. A line he hadn't noticed forming. "Are you okay?"

Jeanette Nolan. He hadn't seen her since the funeral service. He eyed the woman's gentle expression, the kindness in her gaze.

"I will be," he answered, and very nearly believed it.

Chapter Nineteen

Nikki swung by the Jeffersons' hardware store for a wide, lightweight bucket and a string of lights. She found a small selection of boxed glass ornaments and bought one, along with hooks. The tree wasn't very big. She didn't need much to fill the branches. She had extra white paper, too, so she'd make cutout snowflakes to hang on the tree and from the window latches. It would be perfect.

Carrying everything to her car, where the tree stuck out from the open trunk like some restrained, wild growth, she plopped her purchases on the passenger seat before getting behind the wheel. She refused to dwell on the three cardboard packing boxes filled with ornaments that had burned up in the apartment, including those which had once belonged to her parents. They were just things, and things were not life. Ornaments from a mom-and-pop hardware store in a wonderful little town made a great start to a new collection.

Back at the cottage, she lugged her purchases inside. The first thing she did was set the tree in the bucket and watered it, then she cut away the netting, gently coaxing the branches to lower. She hung the wreath on the cottage door outside from a nail she'd noticed in place that morning. Once back inside, Nikki stood a few minutes breathing in the wonderful scent from the evergreen, enjoying the lingering residue from woodsmoke mingling with the balsam's scent.

Woodsmoke was not the same as the searing smoke from many burning materials melding together. Plastics, varnished furniture, cloth, paint, and who knew what else. That had been horrible. This, the blended scents she experienced in her new, temporary home, was pleasant, homey, heartwarming. It didn't conjure fear, only contentment.

Suddenly, she wondered where Rory found his contentment. Or if he just didn't. One day he would. Not because of her. Not through anyone's efforts to drag him there. The steady presence from family and friends helped, certainly, but in the end, it was up to him.

Feeling somewhat ravenous, she ate leftovers from Thanksgiving dinner after putting the strung lights on the tree and plugging them in for effect. She'd freed the ornaments from the box and spread them out on the floor to peruse while she chewed. Between bites, she visually picked the perfect spot for a particular ornament and hung it. Except for the paper snowflakes, by the time Nikki finished her slowly masticated meal, the tree's decoration was finished. Her phone rang.

"Perfect timing," she said out loud, and answered the unknown number. Not something she usually did, letting those calls go to voice mail to be listened to later if legit, and avoiding spam if they weren't. "Hello?"

"Nikki?" said a voice. A very familiar voice. A voice she hadn't anticipated hearing again. Ever.

"Ted," Nikki responded in flat tones, despite the sudden churning in her stomach. "Did you get a new number?"

"I'm calling from work."

Slowly, Nikki lowered her bottom into the camp chair and switched the phone call to speaker, settling the phone on her leg. "Are your parents okay?" Funny, how one's mind went to the worst. Yet, how could it not. Why else would he reach out?

"They're fine, Nikki. I'm not calling with bad news."

She waited in silence.

"You still there?"

"Yes," she said. "What's up?"

"Don't be that way," he muttered at her continuing tone.

Nikki released a sigh. "Ted, just tell me why you're calling."

"You remember Cynthia's friend Carol?"

Barely. Nikki remembered Cynthia far better. Cynthia, Ted's new girlfriend who had moved across the country with him. Settled in with him, quite like they weren't so brand new as he'd claimed.

"The name's familiar," Nikki said.

"It doesn't really matter if you remember her, I guess. But she mentioned to Cynthia the fire at the apartment complex. I'm so sorry. Are you okay?"

Unexpectedly moved by the concern in his voice, Nikki blinked back tears. "I wasn't hurt. I actually wasn't home, but I lost everything except what I had in my car."

Now, it was his turn to be silent. "I'm sorry," he said again after a few seconds.

Nikki's fingernails began to scratch at the chair's canvas, almost of their own accord. "It's not your fault, Ted. I'm okay. No one was hurt in the fire. It was a loss of…things."

"I suppose that's a positive spin on the whole tragedy. Good for you."

Squeezing her eyes shut, Nikki counted backward from ten, speaking far before she reached one. "Well, thanks for checking on me. I appreciate it."

"You promise you're okay?"

Her breath exploded.

"Nikki?"

"I'm fine, Ted. I'm fine. I'm temporarily living in another state where I went for a job. I like it here."

"Good for you," he repeated. "Is there another guy in your life?"

Nikki stared down at the phone in disbelief. "Not that it's any of your business, but no," she lied. Yes, lied, because another guy was in her life. Not in the way Ted meant, but surely tied to it in an inextricable, almost fateful way. "If that's all, I really have to go," Nikki added, wanting him off the phone.

"Okay. Okay, but—"

"I hope you had a nice Thanksgiving. Enjoy your Christmas and—"

"Wait!"

She clenched her hand. "Yes?"

"May I call you again?"

Nikki pulled her lips in between her teeth and released them with a small, popping noise. "No. Take care, Ted." She hung up.

Her whole body felt tense. Not a good sign. How could she still be so angry with him? She sometimes wondered how Rory continued to feel his grief so strongly, and yet here she was, livid with anger, a virulent emotion over something nowhere near as devastating.

Jumping up from the chair, she grabbed paper and scissors and began folding and cutting in the way she remembered making snowflakes from years ago. Except it wasn't working out. Every time she unfolded one, she'd cut it wrong, making them pieces of snowflakes, or jagged circles, or some other indication she really, really shouldn't have a sharp object in her hands right then.

She dropped the scissors on the counter when her phone rang again. Seeing Gina's name, she answered with relief straightaway. "Gina, hi!"

"Hi, Nikki. Nice Thanksgiving?"

"Very. How about you?"

"Quiet. The way I like it."

Nikki smiled. "I can understand that, after how busy you are leading up to it."

"Are you in the middle of anything?"

"Decorating my tree. It's almost finished and the last part, cutting out paper snowflakes, isn't going too well." She chuckled.

"So, you could use a break? How about meeting me for coffee now?"

Nikki glanced at the clock. "Now? Aren't you in the middle of your work day?" She heard Gina's laugh in response.

"I take Black Friday off every year. Leave it all to my staff. No one's knocking down the door for baked goods the day after they've stuffed themselves."

Gina's easy humor was helping. Nikki's respiration steadied. She considered herself pretty easy-going, normally. Hearing from Ted had thrown her out of sorts, especially his request to call her again. Why? Were things not going the way he'd hoped with Cynthia?

Feeling her jaw starting to tense again, she suggested a change in plan to Gina. "Would you be able to go out this evening? We could have dinner."

"With or without alcohol?" Gina asked.

"With works. Where?"

"There's a pub in town, on the point. You might have passed it coming in and out."

Nikki had noticed several times what appeared to be a converted, nineteenth-century home with a quaint green wooden sign above the massive front door. The tavern was called The Sitting Duck. There had to be a story behind a name like that one.

"Sure," Nikki said. "I think it's been calling to me."

Gina laughed again. "Meet you there at, say, seven?"

"Seven works," Nikka answered. "I'll see you there!"

Gina hung up. Smiling, Nikki retrieved the scissors and started anew on the snowflakes, imagining with anticipation a night out. She could scarcely remember the last one she'd had.

*   *   *

Waiting outside The Sitting Duck for Gina, Nikki studied the architecture, wishing she'd worn jeans rather than leggings as a sudden cold wind blew up past her boots and into her coat. Shaking back her sleeve, she glanced at her mother's watch, thankful again she'd been wearing it the day everything burned. The hair-thin minute hand pointed directly at "twelve." Nikki suspected Gina made a habit of being prompt. When Nikki heard her name, she knew she was right, and turned to the woman with a smile.

Gina startled her with a quick, affectionate hug. Nikki returned it and stepped back, grinning and pointing at the pub's sign. "You'll have to explain that to me when we get inside."

"Happily," said Gina. "And if I forget, there's a framed explanation hanging on the wall."

Nikki laughed. "Clever move. Nip rumor and conjecture in the bud."

"Sometimes rumor and conjecture is half the fun. Although, I have to say, the real reason is just as entertaining in this case."

Intrigued, Nikki followed Gina inside. She spotted a framed picture with something written below hanging in the foyer. Nikki decided not to linger there reading it. She and Gina passed into a bar area filled with singles, obvious couples, and an entire family, judging by the resemblance. Regular tables lined one wall and several high-top tables had been scattered so as not to impede traffic. A couple of open doors to the bar's right led into converted rooms, perhaps for events or for quieter dining, but Gina turned left. Nikki understood why a moment later. Another, larger room led off in that direction with more tables. These, too, were nearly filled, but the area was much quieter than the main bar, yet not as cut off as the others she had glimpsed.

It seemed the place to be on a Friday night, especially, Nikki figured, the Friday after Thanksgiving. She wondered if they'd get a table, after all. However, Gina appeared to have anticipated the same thing and had called ahead.

The hostess grinned at Gina, then looked at Nikki. "We don't do this for everyone," she whispered, winking. A server hustled over to a table that had been left uncleaned and filled with dishes to deter anyone sitting at it. After swiftly clearing the surface and wiping it down, he waved them toward the chairs.

"Thanks, Beth," Gina said to the woman as they headed to their seats. Beth followed behind and set their menus down.

"You're very welcome," she said, and departed.

Nikki eased into her chair. "It didn't even occur to me it might be hard to get a table here."

"Why? Because we're a small town?"

Nikki jerked her gaze from the menu she'd been retrieving to Gina's face. The woman's dark brown eyes sparkled with mischief. "No," Nikki answered, smiling ruefully. "Because I don't get out much and tend to forget such things."

Grabbing her own menu, Gina nodded. "We might have to rectify that. Not that I'm much for late nights. I get up way too early. Still, if you stick around long enough, you might find a lot you enjoy in Connor Falls."

"I am sticking around," Nikki said. "Through the New Year. I thought I mentioned that."

Gina didn't look up from perusing her menu. "You did. I meant longer."

Nikki stilled. Her mind went to Rory and her cheeks heated. "Work should be coming up in Brewster, and several other jobs are lining up as well."

"The chicken salad panini with the roasted red peppers is delicious," Gina said, turning her menu toward Nikki and tapping her fingernail on the listing. "And I was thinking you need a home. I heard some of your story from Tessa, as you know. Personally, though, even though you've been here only a short time, there's a big difference in you from the woman I met in my bakery that first day and now."

Sucking in a short, quiet breath through her nostrils, Nikki stared at her table companion. "You don't know me, Gina."

Gina returned her attention to her menu. "I know you well enough and would certainly like to know you better. We all would. You've made a positive impression on those who've met you, believe me. Plus, I've had a look at your website. You travel for work. It's right there on the 'about me' page. And this is a really great place to live. That's all I'm saying."

Nikki's lips twisted. She turned her eyes to her menu without reading it. The server arrived to take their order. Nikki asked for the panini, not bothering to look at anything else. Gina requested the same. When asked what they would like to drink, Gina decided on a white wine.

"Water," said Nikki. "And cranberry juice and peach schnapps over ice. Do you have peach schnapps?"

The server nodded.

"Skip the wine," said Gina. "I'll have one of those, too. Feels more festive."

They both watched the young man walk away. Gina turned to Nikki first. "I'm sorry. I've been told more than once I can be a bit too forward. You do seem happy here, though. I'm not saying you weren't before. But you were certainly…anxious, maybe?"

Nikki filled her lungs and slowly, ever so slowly, let the air out. "I was," she said. "I admit that. And I'm happy here. I admit that, too. But what you're suggesting is a big change."

"Is it, though?" Gina countered. "You've already made the move. You'd only have to make it permanent. What has occurred in your life has, in its way, set you free to do whatever the heck you want and need."

"You sound envious," Nikki said.

"Maybe I am. And maybe I'm not. I like it here. No, I love it here. I have a business and friends and a lifetime of memories, some bad, but mostly good. I'm set in my ways, I've made my life into what I want from it, and yes, sometimes I wish for something else. But I wish for that something else right here. Where are you from originally, Nikki?"

"Too many places to count," Nikki answered, lifting the glass the server had set on the table while she was talking. She took a deep swallow from the ice-cold water. He'd also positioned one by Gina's elbow. After a moment, Gina drank, too.

"Way too many," Nikki added. "We moved around a lot when I was a kid."

"And maybe what I'm noticing is a need for roots. Sorry. I don't mean to be sticking my nose in where it doesn't belong, as the saying goes."

"Don't worry about it. If I seem a little prickly, it's not because of you. Well, it is, but you're not saying anything offensive. It's just making me…think."

"Thinking's always good." Gina raised her water up in a salute. Laughing, Nikki held hers across the table and they clinked glasses.

"To new friends," Nikki said.

Chapter Twenty

Nikki got back to the cottage much later than expected. In order not to disturb the Jeffersons with the glare on their front window, she turned her headlights off before pulling into the driveway, parking in her designated space by the light from the motion sensor fixture on the barn. She'd only had the one drink, and was glad of it, because a cold weather fog had formed over the landscape, drifting into the roadways.

Gina had given her a lot to think about. Nikki suspected she just did this with people. She probably read them all as easily as she'd read Nikki, and then spoke her mind. Not in a prying, interfering way. Not really. She seemed to possess a knack for turning a person's thoughts inward, though. Hers, at any rate. But stay in Connor Falls?

She huffed out a heavy breath and unlocked the cottage door. Balsam scented the air inside. She'd left the small lamp above the kitchen counter turned on. The low-wattage bulb cast a dim glow over the room, somehow managing to glimmer along the glass ornaments. The tiny paper snowflakes on the tree shifted in the breeze from the closing door. Nikki plugged the tree lights in, switched off the lamp, and lowered herself coat and all into the camp chair. She stared at her little Christmas tree and smiled, allowing peace to settle in. A short-lived peace most likely. Her life had changed and she still had decisions to make. But right now, the holiday season had begun. She adored her rented space, adored the Jeffersons, liked the people she'd met in Connor Falls—Gina and Tessa and others. Rory.

Well, Rory she liked a bit more. Or at least differently. Their long-ago connection had much to do with that. Their recent connection, too. Slouched in the camp chair, Nikki closed her eyes, tried not to dwell on him, but her thoughts got stuck there. On Rory's eyes, on the appealing timbre to his voice, on his struggles, on his beautiful talent. On his patience while giving her a refresher with woodworking tools. On his smile when grief was overruled.

Finally, exasperated, she stood and yanked off her coat, climbed the stairs, got undressed and quickly pulled on her sleep pants and tee shirt. She threw a bulky, baggy sweatshirt over top for extra warmth before slipping beneath cold sheets. The heavy quilt would warm her soon enough, trap her own heat and wrap it around her. The way a body beside her would.

The tree lights made a glowing pattern on the ceiling above the narrow stairwell. Nikki considered going down to unplug them, but left them burning because somehow their gentle light felt like company.

*　*　*

Over the weekend, Nikki helped Sheila drag

boxes filled with Christmas decorations down from the attic. She didn't mind doing it. In fact, she was quite happy to assist, especially when Sheila opened the boxes for a quick look inside to coordinate her decorating plans. The woman had written a detailed inventory on the outside, but she said she needed more than words before beginning to remove anything from the boxes.

Nikki enjoyed the stories that went with many of the items. She missed her mother, even after all this time, and the hours she spent talking with Sheila about memories soothed an ache she hadn't realized she still carried around inside. Nikki couldn't help but wonder if, in return, her presence in this tradition temporarily filled for Sheila the emptiness left by Kat's passing. She hoped so. Sheila and Pete had been nothing but kind. It would be nice to give something back in this small way.

"Rory's almost finished here," Sheila commented, her eyes on Nikki. Nikki continued picking up and folding discarded newspaper.

"You'll miss having him underfoot, I'm sure," Nikki said.

"I will."

She seemed to be waiting for something more from Nikki. Nikki ignored the look, stretching her hand to point at a smaller box in the nearest, larger one. "What's that?"

Shiela leaned forward, lifting her chin, and squinting down. She reached past Nikki and drew the box out. "Open it," she said, handing the worn, white carton to Nikki.

Nikki pulled the flaps back, revealing what

appeared to be a snow globe. Carefully, she pulled the heavy piece out and lifted it to the dimming light through the window. The liquid-filled glass held inside a snowy mountain village. The base had been exquisitely carved from wood, possibly cherry. Nikki felt a tiny shape against her palm and quickly glanced beneath at the mechanism for the music box.

"May I?" she asked. "I'll be careful not to overwind it."

Sheila nodded agreement. Nikki turned the key only one full rotation, then set the snow globe on the floor between them. Delicate and sweet, a familiar tune she couldn't name filled the air between them.

"That's lovely," Nikki said. "Really quite beautiful. Where did you get it?"

"It was a gift from Kat."

Nikki swallowed at the emotion in Sheila's voice.

"She got it for me from Hannah's, way back when. Before she got married, I think, although I could be wrong. Hannah's used to purchase snow globes from a company that has since gone out of business. They were always extraordinary."

"I can see that." Nikki bent forward to peer more closely at the feature inside. "Did Kat buy it for you for the song or the snowy village?"

"The village," Sheila said. "I love the snow. The song became special with the gift."

Nikki looked up and smiled at her. At that moment, the front door opened and Pete's voice boomed through the house. Nikki slipped the snow globe into its carton and back into the box before standing up. Pete entered the study where they'd brought all the boxes from the attic.

"Getting ready to start?" he asked his wife. Sheila walked over to him and kissed him lightly on the cheek, the gesture casual yet somehow intimate. Nikki reached for her coat.

"Thanks, Sheila, for sharing all this with me."

"Thanks for your help," Sheila countered. Pete cleared his throat.

"I'm not chasing you out," he said.

"I know. I have some things to do anyway. Enjoy—" she glanced toward the clock, "your evening."

Back in the cottage, she watered the tree, plugged in the lights, and turned on her laptop, opening an online program from which she streamed music. Shortly, low-volume Christmas songs drifted through the room while she built a small fire in the fireplace. Not too big. She didn't want to dry out the evergreen. Once flames licked along the wood, she made a quick dinner and sat down near the warmth to eat it.

Nikki had always been okay on her own. That might have added to Ted's dissatisfaction, too, because, yeah, he needed her to need him. Wanting to be with him wasn't quite enough. She supposed it left too much to chance. Basically, want rather than need meant he possessed no guarantee she'd tolerate his behavior no matter what, making him insecure in the relationship. And if nothing else, she learned through life never to allow someone to shortchange her. In turn, she gave the same consideration. If a man didn't possess the character to meet the challenge, so be it.

Feeling suddenly irritated, Nikki set her empty plate on the floor beside her chair and crossed her arms over her chest. She watched the snowflakes turn on the branch ends in the warm air from the fire. A rather charming dance, really. She hadn't planned it that way. Pushing up from the chair, she grabbed her phone and took a short video of the twirling paper with the Christmas music playing in the background, then sent it to Sammy. A half minute later Sammy responded.

Adorable. Is that what you've been doing with your spare time?

Yep, Nikki texted back.

You haven't met any hot guys in smalltown America?

Nikki pursed her lips, eyes narrowing at the phone. *Not why I'm here. I came for work. And to get away.*

You're away. And you're not working now. Go do something fun.

For a split second, Nikki considered responding with something about Rory, but there was too much to say. Instead, she typed: *I'll think about it.*

Don't think, Sammy texted. *Just do. And let me know!*

Okay. Love you, she answered and tossed the cell phone back on the counter. Before she reached her chair, her phone chirped again. Nikki snatched it up, looked at the single word.

Hi.

Not Sammy. Rory.

Hello, Nikki texted him. *How are you?*

Good. Are you busy?

Should she be honest? Of course. *Not busy. What's up?*

I'm at Luke's and Lydia asked if I would text you so she could ask you something.

Nikki's mouth curved up realizing Rory was at his brother's house again. Her smile turned into a grin as she pictured Lyddie coercing her uncle to do her bidding. *Sure,* she typed hastily. *Tell her to ask away.*

A couple minutes passed. Nikki wandered back over to the fire with the phone, lowering herself into the camp chair. She could see the moving dots indicating typing on the other end and wondered if Lyddie was dictating to Rory or entering the query herself. When the question finally popped up, she laughed out loud.

Costume caroling? Nikki typed back. *What is that?*

Although she couldn't imagine why, the fact Lydia wanted her to go caroling touched Nikki's heart. She'd only been with the girl for one short evening, but thinking back on that night, she and Lydia had sung together a song playing on the television. Nikki really needed more details before agreeing. She glanced at the moving dots, waiting for a response. Abruptly, they stopped. The phone rang.

"Lyddie?" Nikki said, answering the call.

"It's me," said Rory. "I'm not that quick on such a tiny keypad. It'll be easier to explain."

In the background she heard Lydia begging.

"Please, Uncle Rory, don't let her say no."

"That's beyond my power to control, Lyds," Rory said to his niece before addressing Nikki again. "Long story short," he explained, and Nikki closed her eyes at the deep timbre of his voice, "Luke has this thing every year the first weekend in December—"

"So, next weekend," Nikki interrupted, just to be sure.

"Right. Next weekend. Anyway, it's to raise money for the Children's Hospital. It's only a couple hours. The profit from the tree sales for that timeframe go to it. People pitch in with baked goods, apple cider, hot chocolate, that sort of thing. Farmers bring their most docile livestock for viewing, usually wearing something seasonal, if you can believe that."

Nikki chuckled.

"Tell her about the caroling," Lydia said, sounding like she'd moved closer to the phone.

"I'm getting there," Rory told Lydia. A chair scuffed the floor as Rory probably stood up to elude his niece's reach. "And there's caroling," he said to Nikki. "The carolers walk around through the whole event singing Christmas songs."

"In costume, Nikki!"

"In costume," Rory repeated for Nikki's benefit. "Actually, anything that looks vaguely Victorian. Some people have real costumes, but the rest wing it."

Nikki considered for several seconds.

"You don't have to," Rory hastened to add.

"Is there a practice beforehand?" Nikki asked.

"I haven't gone caroling in years."

"There is. The event's on Saturday, and Friday night practice takes place in Luke's barn."

"At seven o'clock!" Lydia called out. "Uncle Rory's going!"

Rory spoke softly when he answered the little girl. "I didn't say that, Lyddie."

Nikki heard Luke's voice in the background. "Let Uncle Rory finish his phone call, okay? Help me get the table set."

"Sorry," Rory said, unnecessarily.

"No need to apologize."

"Anyway, that's what Lydia wanted to ask you."

"It's very sweet that she wants me there—"

"But you don't have to do it."

Nikki inhaled. "Tell you what. I'll go if you go."

"What?"

"I'll go if you go. Have you ever done this?"

"Before," he stated rather flatly. Nikki understood.

"Then it'll do us both good," she said. "I'll start getting presentable attire ready and you show up with whatever you used to wear. If I don't see you here beforehand, I'll see you at Luke's on Friday." Nikki held her breath.

"Okay," he said after a lengthy silence. "I'll see you then." He didn't sound enthused. Even so, Nikki hung up grinning like a Cheshire cat.

In the morning, Nikki had a long call with a shop owner in a larger, nearby town. The man had been referred to Nikki by Tessa. He required a professional rearrangement of a display he'd set up himself. After reviewing the photos he texted her, Nikki agreed to come by the next day. As she set the phone on the counter, she spotted Rory through the window, heading toward his truck. Not bothering with her coat, she hurried out the door to speak with him.

"Rory!"

He glanced back and away, then back again, stopping in his tracks.

"Rory," Nikki said again, "I'm sorry."

His dark brows arched. "For what?"

Coming to a halt beside him, Nikki tipped her head back to look at his face, shielding her eyes from the afternoon sun with her hand. "Making you agree to the caroling."

"You didn't *make* me," Rory countered.

"Didn't I?"

"Nope. The word no is in my vocabulary. It is, however, a little harder to say 'no' to Lydia. After I hung up with you the other night, she wouldn't relent. In a sweet way, but she still wore me down. Prior to that, yeah, I had been inclined to back out from my agreement with you. But as you said, if you go, I go."

Nikki scuffed her boot in the gravel. "Okay. Good. Because I've been practicing. Singing along to the radio."

Rory frowned a little. "Are you saying you wouldn't go if I didn't?"

"Heck no," said Nikki. "Lydia would never let me off the hook."

He laughed, reached out, squeezed her arm.

Despite the chilly air, his hand was warm on her sleeve. She felt its absence as soon as he pulled his fingers away. "I'm actually finished here," he said, jerking his chin toward the Jeffersons' home. "Until something else comes up, I suppose."

"Sheila said she and Pete lived in the cottage at one point, while the house was being worked on. But they've had the house for years, yes?"

He nodded. "They bought the house almost thirty-five years ago, I believe. They've been fixing it up bit by bit for a long while. Sheila and Pete were in the cottage briefly while the plumbing and electric were getting a re-do."

"It's a beautiful place," Nikki said. "And a wonderful home."

When he didn't answer right away, Nikki looked back at him over her shoulder. His expression made her cheeks heat. She planned to fully blame the color on the cold, if he mentioned it.

"Nikki, I—"

"Dinner?" she cut in.

"Excuse me?"

"Dinner. Maybe dinner out would be a good way to celebrate a job well done."

He didn't answer. Nikki shifted her weight from one foot to the other. "Or not," she said.

"Nikki, my evenings are full the rest of the week."

His gaze met hers. Nikki couldn't tell what she saw there. She felt…scrutinized. Her blush deepened.

"Got it," she said. "I've got a job in the next town over tomorrow. Looking forward to that." She started backing away.

"Nikki."

She stopped.

"I'll see you Friday. I'll be the guy in the top hat and scarf."

Nikki gave him a crooked smile. "Probably not the only one. Maybe you should put a flower in your lapel, too, just to make sure I recognize you."

"That'll be on Saturday, when you really need to know who you're standing next to."

"I'll remember that. See you Friday." She waved and hurried back into the cottage before she made an utter fool of herself.

*　　*　　*

Two hours later, Rory shifted on the hard seat beneath his hips, sighed and admitted to all present in the church basement, "I didn't want to turn Nikki down. Another meal with her would have been nice. I suppose the fact I'm admitting such a thing to myself is another step in the right direction?"

The people seated in the circle all responded with some form of agreement. The group leader, Deirdre, cleared her throat. "We all follow our own path when recovering from loss," she said. "There is no right or wrong direction. The question is, do you feel better having realized something positive in your life? Or worse?"

Rory thought a moment. "Better," he said. "Definitely better."

Deirdre smiled. "Good."

Rory inclined his head and lifted the donut in his hand to his mouth, taking a bite without answering. He followed this up with sips from his coffee. He hadn't had a meal before leaving the house. What he really wanted to do was scarf down the pastry in his hand, but he took his time. He remembered when he'd first starting coming to the meetings, anything he'd eaten had tasted like sandpaper. He remembered when he stopped coming, too, because anything resembling hope had seemed a betrayal.

Releasing a breath, he glanced around at all the others gathered here to work through their grieving. They lightheartedly called themselves Grievers Anonymous. Rory couldn't remember the actual name. It didn't matter. Gina Hart had suggested the group to him one day. He had no idea her connection to it, who she'd lost, or if it was even a death she grieved. She had pointed out in that brief conversation how grief resulted from any number of things and sometimes a person needed a little help getting through. Especially in the holiday season. Knowing there was a joy you were supposed to feel sometimes cut a vicious swath through your soul.

On the way home, he came to a decision. A small one. Small steps, that's what they'd all discussed and had loosely agreed to as "homework." He felt like he should be taking big steps now, but big or small, forward motion was the key. Inside the house, he climbed the stairs straight to the linen closet, yanked the door open. He stared at the folded piles inside and chose a set of sheets with a holiday design. Not Kat's favorite, but definitely at one point his. He also pulled out a blanket, the one his sister had removed and washed long ago after the funeral, and he'd never replaced.

Thinking about his sister gave him a twang. Jen lived in Washington and came East with the kids and her husband a few times a year. He talked to her in between often enough, and to the kids, and even Al. They were sometimes stilted conversations, but occasionally a bit more like the ones he remembered, the ones they had when they and Luke and their folks physically got together. He rarely initiated the calls since he'd lost Kat, though. That would be another small step. Even if he had to put a reminder in his phone, he'd be the one to call them.

Rory yanked out his cell phone and immediately made a reminder for late the following evening, accounting for the three-hour time difference. Phone back in his pocket, he went into the bedroom to make up the bed. For a long moment, a ridiculously long moment, he stared at the bare mattress, bedding clutched against his chest. He inhaled deeply several times, expecting the grief he'd known for so long. Instead, Rory experienced sadness mixed with anticipation. He decided not to examine his emotions too closely and instead made up the bed, standing back when done to study the effect. On him, on the empty room. His lips curled up with a memory that made him feel good, not bad. After showering, he climbed beneath the covers, the motion-activated light on the garage shining through the window and across the quilt. No doubt an animal had caused the fixture to react. Rory started drifting into slumber before the bulb went dark.

Chapter Twenty-One

Nikki wrapped a scarf around her neck and pulled up her hood. Her breath frosted in the frigid air. Hopefully, Luke's barn had a large heater, at least where they'd be practicing. It would be interesting, this. Nikki had no idea what they would even be singing. Maybe the list was the same each year and those who returned to carol were well-versed. Tucking her hand-sewn bonnet into her pocket, she headed for her car. Rory's parking spot had been empty since Tuesday. She hadn't asked Sheila about him. He'd told Nikki he'd finished up in the house. He had no reason for frequent returns now.

Still, Nikki missed him. Stupid, really. Yet he had been making daily appearances in her life since her arrival. She'd see him shortly, though. Feel him out. See how he was doing. Nothing more. No dinner invites. The new year was approaching and she had decisions to make. She wouldn't complicate them further.

When Nikki pulled up outside the barn at Luke's Tree Farm, she noted multiple cars parked in the lot near the slightly open door, the interior and exterior lights gleaming across their hoods. What she did not see was a very familiar pickup truck. She glanced at the time before pulling in at the row's far end. Exiting her car, she heard voices from inside the barn and started in their direction.

A footstep fell behind her. "Nikki?"

Rory's deep timbre, followed instantly by another, higher-pitched call. "Nikki!" Lydia squealed.

Nikki jerked around. Rory stood beside Lyddie, who clutched a cat against her chest. She raised her arms in their pink coat sleeves and held the small animal up for Nikki to see. Not a kitten, but still young, not fully grown into its skin.

Nikki reached out to pet the cat's ginger ears, avoiding Rory's gaze. "What's its name?" she asked Lydia.

"Frank," Lydia answered.

"Frank? Like the man who works for your dad?"

"Uh-huh," the girl answered with a vigorous nod.

"Doesn't that get confusing?"

"Nah," said Lydia. "Frank—the man—knows who I'm talking to, and Frank, the cat," she added, cuddling the purring animal against her neck, "doesn't know his name yet, so he's not answering anyway."

"Got it," said Nikki.

"He likes me to sing to him, so I'll hold him while we practice." Lydia darted with the cat toward the open door, glancing back before going inside. Nikki followed her, Rory ambling at her side.

"Sweet cat," Nikki said conversationally. "Has she had it long?"

"She found it in the barn two days ago. They come and go. Mice are plentiful in there. But this one didn't seem wild. Luke asked around if anyone lost a kitten, but so far, the cat has gone unclaimed."

"Except by Lyddie."

"Except by Lyddie," he agreed.

They were both silent then until they got inside. Nikki spotted Tessa and Gina, greeting them both, followed by Luke, who introduced her to the rest too quickly for her to remember all the names. About sixteen townsfolk had gathered in the barn. None of them wore anything even vaguely Victorian. Rory remained hatless. Nikki kept her bonnet in her pocket. It made sense no one dressed until the actual caroling performance. She should have realized.

Gina stepped forward, handing Nikki a sheaf of copied sheet music covered by a ruby-red folder. Rory retrieved his from nearby. Seeing the lyrics definitely helped. All the songs were familiar and popular, which meant she wouldn't have any problem singing along. Good thing, because they got right into it as soon as the singers shuffled into various positions across the floor. Lyddie sat on a nearby wooden table, legs dangling over the side, her cat in her lap. They started with the top sheet and went from there, beginning with *Jolly Old Saint Nicholas*. The sheets were stapled at the top, preventing them getting mixed up. Someone had been well prepared. Most likely Gina or Luke.

They spent an hour or so practicing, paused to drink fresh apple cider, and practiced some more. At one point, Rory appeared beside Nikki again and stayed there. Nikki felt his presence in more ways than she expected, distracting and yet welcome. He possessed a lovely baritone, singing, as they all did, without any self-conscious restraint. A luscious scent filled the air from evergreen trimmings piled for the taking along one wall. The fragrance mixing with the aroma floating up from the cinnamon-sprinkled cider prompted Nikki to comment, "It feels like Christmas in here."

And it did. Warm, welcoming, communal, quietly joyful, purposeful, and with a bonus musical accompaniment. In a low voice, Rory agreed. Luke caught his words. He sent his brother a pleased look.

A short time later, they all flipped the pages to the last song. Nikki heard Rory exhale. It was an odd sound. Nikki glanced up at him. He took a step back.

"You okay?" she whispered.

He swallowed, cartilage bobbing visibly in his throat. He'd yanked his scarf aside earlier in the barn's warmth. "Fine," he said. "I'd forgotten though. This is—"

"Kat's song," Luke finished for him. "Her favorite Christmas song," he explained to Nikki before speaking again to Rory. "I'm sorry. I should have taken it out."

"No," said Rory in a firm tone, "you shouldn't have. Quit letting me off the hook, Luke. We sing it, just like any of the others."

"For Kat," Nikki said without thinking, "and for you."

Silence settled over the singers. Nikki looked around.

"Have I said something wrong?" she asked.

"Not at all," Rory answered. "Let's do it."

Lydia appeared at Rory's other side. She slipped her hand in his. Cat Frank remained on the table, watching through golden eyes. "Yeah, Uncle Rory," she said. "Let's do it."

They sang *I Wonder as I Wander,* always a moving song for Nikki. She found herself turning away, blinking back tears. Once they had finished, Rory cleared his throat and lifted his hand, two fingers loosely raised, like they were in a classroom.

"Didn't we used to finish up with *Carol of the Bells*?" he asked.

"It's not the easiest to sing, and with three new singers joining us I thought maybe we should let that one go," Luke said.

"I'm game," said Nikki, leaning forward and looking around for the other two newbies. "A finale should be upbeat and rather spectacular, yes?"

"Agreed," said an obvious couple in unison.

"And if we can't manage it," Nikki added, "we three will just move our mouths and pretend a lot."

Her comment was met with laughter. Practice continued following her declaration until nearly eleven o'clock, ending up with a quick route for the carolers outlined on a chalkboard where the animal stalls and various craft and food vendors had been mapped out. Someone commented on Luke's efficiency.

"He always has been," Rory said with a smile. "My little brother puts me to shame."

"Who are you calling 'little'?" Luke shot back, grinning.

The gathering broke up quickly following the affectionate exchange. Saturday's event ran from two o'clock until six, and they all promised to meet in the barn wearing appropriate dress at three-forty-five. Caroling began at four. Standing among the group, Nikki was again struck by the sensation she belonged, as though no one here was a stranger to her. She felt at ease. At home.

But she wasn't home. Not unless she chose to live in Connor Falls, and she had a lot more thinking to do before she jumped all the way to that conclusion.

Outside, everyone said goodnight. Luke

carried a sleepy Lydia and her docile cat back toward the house after closing the barn door. Rory jerked a thumb over his shoulder. "I'm parked up by the house," he said to Nikki.

"Okay. I'll see you tomorrow, then." Nikki began backing toward her parked vehicle, one foot behind the other, while Rory dogged her movements from a dozen feet away. Eventually they both stopped, Nikki when she bumped into her car and Rory, upon seeing her do it.

"I haven't been avoiding you, Nikki," he said.

"I didn't think you had been," Nikki answered, not altogether truthfully. "And you really don't owe me any explanations for your time."

"I know."

"So, I'll see you here tomorrow." She met his eyes. He stared back for a long moment. Too long. Nikki's face heated. Her body felt warm under her coat and sweater. He seemed to realize his prolonged gaze and blinked, taking a step away.

"Tomorrow," he said. Smiling, he nodded and spun on his heel. He strode a bit self-consciously up the incline toward Luke's house. Halfway up the hill he turned and waved. Realizing she should have been in her car already Nikki gave a quick wave back and hurried around to the driver's side. She climbed in behind the wheel, peering through the passenger window toward Rory's retreating, shadowed form.

Something had changed for him. A good change. A change in a positive direction. A change, though, that left her confused about her part in it.

Chapter Twenty-Two

Nikki had purchased extra fabric and by lunch time on Saturday had whipped up a long skirt using a glue gun rather than sewing all the stitches by hand. She had two coats, the dressier one a dark wool rather than the fiberfill ski-type, and went well enough with the skirt and bonnet. For added effect, she prepared a muff for her hands from faux fur. Eyeing herself piecemeal with a mirror she lifted from the wall, she decided she'd achieved the proper Victorian vibe. Sheila confirmed it when she came to the door.

"You look great! Good job. If I'd known you were going all out, I'd have loaned you my sewing machine. Did you sew all that by hand?"

Nikki pointed over her shoulder where the unplugged glue gun lay on a piece of newspaper, cooling. Sheila laughed.

"I'm not wearing it for a night on the town, so it should hold up," Nikki joked.

"Don't be too sure. Everyone involved in the event usually heads to the pub afterward. Here, I brought you a mini-pumpkin pie. I'm going to be selling them at a table, so I've got to run."

Sheila shoved a small, delicious smelling pie into Nikki's hand and hurried away. "I'll see you shortly!" the woman called over her shoulder.

Nikki waved and shut the door, holding the pie to her nose. Her stomach rumbled. She hadn't stopped to eat any lunch. Taking the pie to the counter, Nikki grabbed a fork and began to eat it standing up, wondering if what Sheila had said was true. Nikki had enjoyed her evening with Gina at The Sitting Duck. Did they go there or somewhere else? Would Rory actually join in, too? Part of her didn't think it likely, but the other part remembered the change in him last night. He might. He just might.

And maybe she shouldn't.

Growling under her breath, she finished off the pie and retrieved leggings from the small dresser to slip on beneath her skirt. She didn't want to be freezing the whole time she strolled with the rest of the group. If she made her way through the crowd beside Rory, she wouldn't be, of course, but she couldn't think about that, anticipate that, look forward to it. She had planned her time at Connor Falls as a respite and to strategize her future. She couldn't be distracted, as much as she liked Rory.

There, she'd admitted her feelings to herself. Again. And wanted to kick herself. Again. Pictured herself kissing him anyway. Holding his hand. Standing close to his body's warmth. Fitting into the circle formed by his arms. Other things.

"Not happening, not happening, not happening," she said out loud while she slipped her feet into her boots. "I can't do that to him," she admitted as she stuffed her phone, her wallet, into her coat pocket, rather than lug her purse along. "I can't do that to me," she added, snatching her keys from the counter.

By the time she headed out to her car, she determined to put as much distance as possible between herself and Rory during the presentation. By the time she eased into her seat behind the wheel, she was pretty sure that wasn't going to happen.

Less than fifteen minutes later, Nikki had parked and was moving among the various vendors and the people gathered for the event. Some she'd met already through her dealings with the townsfolk, but the rest she didn't recognize. Just like any other town, a person couldn't know everybody. Yet here, it didn't seem to matter so much.

"Are you a singer?" a woman considerably younger than Nikki asked from behind a display covered with lovely, handmade earrings.

"Purporting to be," Nikki answered, smiling. "I'll do my best."

"Yeah," the vendor said, "I don't remember you from last year. First time? I've always wanted to do it, but I don't have the nerve."

"First time here, yes. And you won't know if

you can if you don't try. Maybe next year for you?"

"Maybe," she responded, her gaze suddenly moving away from Nikki's. Eyebrows arching, the young woman's lips curved. Cheeks already pink from cold deepened in color. "May I help you? Would you like to see something?"

"Not today, thanks," a deep voice said behind Nikki. Nikki turned slowly to face Rory.

"Hi," she said.

Taking her hand, he tucked it into his arm and turned toward the barn. "It's three-forty-five. Gina asked me to fetch you."

"Like a wandering child," Nikki answered, picking up on what might be Gina's matchmaking. Gina could have sent anyone after her. It didn't have to be Rory. "Got it."

"No, not like a child," he said at her tone. "Are you all right?"

"I'm fine. Just nervous," she lied.

"Great job with the outfit."

She glanced up at his head. "You, too. A hat and scarf go a long way."

"I don't sew," he said.

"I didn't," she responded. "Hot glue."

His laughter boomed off the barn wall, turning heads. Nikki hadn't heard him laugh this hard since the evening they spent in each other's company in Manhattan. Amused bouts had been cut through with the sadness she occasionally saw revealed in his eyes. She'd forgotten those dark moments. Maybe that was why she'd stayed with him, kept talking, kept making him laugh.

Yes, because even then she cared about him.

About a stranger. Her life had changed. So had his. And she still cared.

Inside the barn, people were making last-minute adjustments to their attire. Lyddie looked endearing in hers. When Nikki said as much, the girl told her Gina had made the hat and skirt. "We match," said Lydia, pointing at Nikki's clothing. They both wore a similar style bonnet and skirt made from blue fabric.

"Yeah, but I bet Gina used a sewing machine on yours," Nikki said, causing a chuckle to erupt from Rory behind her. At Lyddie's confused expression, Nikki explained, "I glued my outfit together."

The girl appeared fascinated by that information and reached out to touch Nikki's skirt. "I can feel it, but I don't think anyone else will notice," she whispered.

"Where's Frank? Cat Frank?" Nikki asked.

Lydia giggled. "In the house. Dad said he might get scared with all the people."

"Sounds about right. Good plan. He'll be warm in there, too."

Luke called everyone's attention. He pointed to water bottles on the table. "Tuck 'em in where you can. They're lukewarm, although probably won't stay that way. We don't want anyone's throats going dry, though." He grinned around at them all. "Thank you for doing this. As always, I appreciate your time and your voices."

Murmured responses as to the cause and Luke's efforts followed. Everyone grabbed a bottle, made sure they had their sheet music, and headed out the door.

Acapella performance always thrilled Nikki. A beautifully minimalist yet complicated and melodic union. Nikki had her favorite groups she listened to, especially during the holidays. She hadn't gone caroling in quite a long time and grinned from sheer joy after every song with the singers Luke's had banded together. It had been decided the night before that Lydia would sing a verse from *Silver Bells* solo. The girl hadn't hesitated then and didn't when the time came. She possessed a stunning voice for one so young and received special applause from the crowd.

The group's members changed places as they walked, to alter the sound, but somehow Rory frequently ended up by Nikki's side. His rich baritone gave her goosebumps. Or maybe it was his nearness. She kept pushing the consideration from her mind, concentrating on the music and the performance. Nikki figured most people in the crowd had been here before and knew what to expect, because most stayed until the very end. The clapping following the finale went on for a good five minutes. Sheila appeared with an envelope for Luke as they were heading back into the barn.

"Sold out," she said with a grin. "Pete's packing up now. I wanted to make sure I got the money to you before I left."

Luke looked like he might say something after his "thank you," but she hurried away before he could. He turned to his brother. "Every year she gives all she's made for the day. The table fee is what's supposed to be the contribution."

"You know Sheila," Rory responded quietly.

"I do."

The exchange was somehow significant in a way Nikki couldn't read. She didn't need to. Not her business. She backed toward the door, preparing to leave. Gina called her.

"Nikki, where do you think you're sneaking off to?"

"To change out of my glued together clothes."

"Tradition is we all go out to the pub after caroling dressed as we are."

"Except me," Lydia said glumly.

"And me," said Luke. "You and I have something special planned. This year we're going to get the decorations up well before Christmas Eve."

"But December just started," Lyddie cried, wide-eyed.

"We were planning to surprise a certain someone, weren't we?"

Lydia jumped down from the table where she'd been sitting. "Right!" She grabbed her father's hand and, with the other, waved at everyone else. "See ya! I had a lot of fun."

Rory volunteered to pull in the tables and lock up the barn. No one would leave without him, causing a delay in exodus, but everything was brought inside within fifteen minutes. People drifted toward their cars while Rory inserted the padlock into the metal doorhandle. Once again, Nikki started backing up. Gina and Tessa stepped around Rory, striding up to her arm in arm.

"Tessa gave me a ride. We'll see you there, Nikki," Gina said. "You, too, Rory," she called over her shoulder. "I'll save you both a seat."

The last ones left standing in the lot, Nikki and Rory stared at each other. "Are you going?" Rory asked her.

She took a deep breath. "I suppose I am."

He nodded. "Okay. So am I."

*　　*　　*

Rory sat in his truck, studying the people coming and going in the pub's parking lot. He recognized some. Many he didn't. It was a popular place with good food and atmosphere. People came from other towns to frequent the establishment. He could expect a certain anonymity, but not total. The time had come to move past hesitation and seclusion. Tessa was right. Kat wouldn't want this for him and neither should he.

Pushing the door open, he climbed out and stood a moment breathing in the crisp air. He had to be honest with himself. He loved fall and winter. The changing leaves, the cooler temperatures, the potential for snow, the holidays with friends and family. And he'd spent more time with both so far this season than he had since Kat passed away. A good sign. A positive sign. All he had to do now was go into the pub, maybe have a beer, maybe something without alcohol. It didn't matter what he drank. What mattered was being himself again.

When he stepped inside, he found Nikki studying the picture on the wall in the foyer. Maybe this was a good sign, too, finding her right there. He walked up next to her.

"What're you looking at?" he asked, even though he could see The Sitting Duck's tale in the frame. He knew it well.

"Cute story," she said, pointing at the female mallard on its nest in the photograph. Below, fancy, calligraphic script recounted the events which had delayed renovation on the old Bradley place from residence to business. "Was there really a duck in the building?"

"Yes, and I should know. I found her. Other work was done until the hatchlings made their way to the stream out back—where the bridge is at the far side of the parking lot?" he added, at her quizzical look. "The owners filed paperwork to change the dba after that."

"Dba?" Nikki echoed. "Oh, doing business as. I should know that." She laughed.

"Are you hovering near the door for a reason? Besides the sitting duck story, I mean."

"I wasn't waiting for you," she answered hastily.

"I didn't think you were."

"Actually, I wasn't sure you'd show up. I'm glad you did."

"Me, too," he said with a slow smile. "And you? Door? Why?"

"I don't know. I might have been thinking about leaving."

He made a guttural noise in his throat and dropped his hand on her shoulder. "If I'm going in, so are you. Come on. Let's have some fun."

Those words coming from his mouth didn't sound quite as absurd as he thought they might. He snagged Nikki's coat sleeve between his thumb and forefinger and tugged her into the main bar area.

The place had been decorated for the holidays with twinkling, warm white lights and a decorated artificial tree in the corner. A very realistic artificial tree. Rory snuck a pinch as he passed to make sure it wasn't live. He couldn't help himself. In his younger years, he'd spent hours on his father's tree farm.

Somehow on a Saturday night, the carolers had managed to snag tables and a couple booths. Upon seeing him and Nikki, all waved them over, calling loudly but good-naturedly. Gina shot a look in Nikki's direction and gave her a broad grin.

"What are you having?" Gina asked her.

"Cranberry juice?" Nikki said. "And I've got it."

"Nope. You're a cheap date. I'll go grab it. Rory?"

Self-consciously, he avoided asking for the same thing and opted for a beer. He pulled a twenty from his pocket and shoved it in Gina's direction as she passed. "Only one. I'm serious. I'm not getting drunk my first night out on the town in, well, a long, long time."

Gina bobbed her head in understanding and slipped away. Rory turned back to Nikki. "There are a couple stools over there. Shall we grab them?"

They did, yanking them closer to where everyone else sat. Someone had ordered appetizers for all to share. Rory added another to their order when the server came over to the table and, as he hadn't eaten since lunch, took a few pretzel bites from the nearest dish before Gina returned with full hands. Someone who had been at Luke's farm spotted the group and she and her friends urged them all to sing. After a brief discussion, Gina and several others good-naturedly agreed, the rest following suit and breaking into *Deck the Halls*. This prompted the buying of another round in return for the song. This quirky holiday tradition was destined to continue at intervals through the night. Rory remembered as much, anyway. Mel and Carter, the owners, had always encouraged the interaction. Seeing Rory with the group now, Mel flashed him a brilliant smile. Rory shrugged and grinned crookedly in response.

"Are you having fun?" Nikki whispered in an aside to him.

"I believe I am," he whispered back.

"Me, too."

He was glad to hear it. He liked Nikki. He liked her a lot. He didn't know quite what this meant in his life at the moment, or where he could go with the knowledge, but admitting it to himself felt good, warming. Hopeful. He smiled at her. "Maybe we—"

Gina tapped on her nearly empty glass with a fork from an appetizer plate. She had recently returned to the table after speaking with someone across the room. "Sorry, all," she said. "I was just told the carolers who are scheduled to sing in the park next Saturday are missing more than half their members due to a last-minute acceptance into some sort of competition. Everyone here is welcome to join in if they'd like. Just let Reece know." She pointed at a gray-haired man standing at the bar, who lifted his hand and waved. "If you're unsure, you can ask him for a business card and give him a call when you decide. I told him there are a lot of commitments this time of year so not to get his hopes up."

Gina uttered the last with a glint in her eye which only grew as many in the group immediately rose and crossed the floor to give Reece their information. Rory didn't move. A second passed before he called over, "Somebody grab me a card."

"Make that two," Gina said, looking pointedly at Nikki.

"Yeah, okay, just in case," Nikki answered.

Rory eyed Nikki, wondering if she had the same suspicion he did. Gina didn't usually butt into people's lives in such an obvious way, but she also possessed an uncanny instinct for recognizing what people needed. What they needed. He didn't want to need anyone again. No offense to Nikki. Or to Kat. Ever.

Dismissing uncertainties, Rory enjoyed the remaining evening, sang with the others, spoke to people he hadn't seen in ages, had a couple more beers. If Nikki happened to be nearby during any exchange, he introduced her. As if she were someone important in his life. Which she was, but maybe not in the exact way revealed in the looks exchanged between those who remembered him from before his self-imposed exile. Worrying the unaccustomed alcohol might be fogging his focus, he switched to water as the night went on. Finally, he announced his intention to head home.

Nikki walked him out. Of course, she did. They

stood a moment on the steps outside, side by side. Their breath co-mingled in the cold air. Nikki looked up at the sky.

"Clear night," she said.

"Snow's on the way," he answered.

"Really?"

"I remember my promise," he said, not totally surprised by his words. "I won't forget."

"Thank you."

That's when it happened. Without thinking, he stepped down to the next step, putting them more at a level, height-wise, and kissed her. A delightful, heated, heady kiss. Her breath rushed out from her nose across his chilled cheek as she pressed closer. But suddenly, she stopped, pulled away. Her eyes were wide, staring into his. He knew right then he'd misread the situation. Made a mistake. A big mistake.

"Nikki, I'm sorry—"

"Don't be. I just—"

"I'm sorry," he said again, apologizing maybe not only to her. He squeezed her hand, let it go, and hurried head down around the building into the parking lot toward his truck.

*   *   *

Nikki stared after Rory, torn between running after him and letting him go. She decided on the latter. He needed time to think. So did she.

Returning inside, Nikki made her way back to the group. They had gathered their outerwear and were singing one last song. Nikki didn't join in, making her way around them to retrieve her own coat. Somehow, the magic in the evening seemed to have popped like a bubble.

Tessa came over to her when the song ended, holding out a business card. "Reese's card," she said. "I'm not sure I'll be able to join in. My hours get crazy this time of year. But you should. It'll be fun."

"I'll think about it," Nikki said, tucking the card into her coat pocket.

"Don't think," Gina said from behind Tessa. "Do."

Nikki had the feeling the bakery owner wasn't talking only about caroling in the park. Nikki nodded. "Okay," she said. "This was great." She pulled some money from her pocket and extended it to Gina. "I assume you're going to settle the bill now. Here's my contribution."

With a thanks and a long, significant look, Gina headed toward the bar. Nikki turned to the rest, who were shoving arms into coat sleeves, wrapping scarfs around necks. "I had a great time tonight," she said. "It was a lot of fun spending the evening with you all."

"Well, we'll see you soon, though," said a woman who'd been introduced as Pamela. "You'll be joining us in the park, right?"

"I might," Nikki hedged.

"You'll have to let Reese know soon, okay? And you'll be there. We know you will. You enjoyed this way too much to skip it."

Nikki nodded and smiled, committing to her enjoyment but nothing more. She slipped out before the rest of them could and made her way to her car.

The ride back to the Jeffersons felt oddly long. When Nikki pulled into the driveway and parked her car, she sat behind the wheel for a time studying the partially hidden cottage through the windshield. Home. Her temporary home. Honestly, she could never live in a place so small on an ongoing basis. Yet, with her possessions gone up in literal smoke, she realized she'd accumulated more than she needed in her apartment. Except for certain items to which she'd felt an emotional attachment, she didn't miss any of it. This, she supposed, was why people lived tiny home lives. Down-sizing. Not enough room to start collecting again. More time to enjoy everything else.

Nikki went inside. She turned on the Christmas tree lights and sat down in the camp chair, her coat hiking up until the collar embraced her jawbone. She started humming some of the evening's tunes beneath her breath, watching the tiny bulbs twinkle in the dark. She thought about Rory's kiss. Really thought about it. Her skin warmed. Could she let it happen again? She didn't know. Would she like it to happen again? Absolutely.

Scrambling up from the chair, she went to her laptop on the kitchen counter and flipped it open to check her email—a habit she couldn't forsake, checking emails before bed. She answered several, including one from Sammy, leaving out a very significant detail from her night. She wasn't ready to share. She didn't want conclusions drawn or advice given. She wanted to hold onto that intimate moment as a very private thing for now. Next came an email she almost deleted as junk. Instead, she opened it. Her breath whistled out.

Someone was offering her a job. A job very far away from Connor Falls.

Chapter Twenty-Three

Nikki received an answer to her responding email by mid-morning. An on-line meeting was scheduled between them for one o'clock. Nikki's social media sharing of Hannah's windows was gaining momentum, apparently. Her pride in her work had never been more evident to Nikki than here, in Connor Falls. Perhaps because she'd risen to get a nearly impossible job completed in record time and loved the results without reservation. She decided then and there to make some changes to her website, putting the windows as background to the main page, as well as where they currently resided in the gallery.

She sat down straightaway to make the alterations, a small fire warm at her back, but not enough to dry out the freshly watered tree. Afterward, she made a Christmas list. She wanted to give small gifts to certain people in town and, having been inside many shops, had an idea which local businesses she'd buy from. She listed names on the left, gifts on the right. Rory's name appeared on top, but she quickly moved it to last. When she finally shut down the computer, the space beside his name remained empty.

Realizing she just had time for a quick shower and to change into something other than a sweatshirt, Nikki headed for the stairs. A knock sounded on the door. A light knock. Sheila, most likely.

The woman greeted her as Nikki opened the door. "Hi! I promised myself I'd never be one of those pestering landlords. And I really don't consider myself a landlord. I had no plans to rent this place out until I came up with them to get Rory to go back home."

Nikki stepped back. "Come on in."

Sheila did, towing a trail of frigid air behind her. Nikki quickly shut the door. The draft rushed into the narrow space between the glass doors on the hearth. The flames hissed and shivered.

"What's that you got there?" Nikki asked, nodding toward Sheila's hand.

"A bag of cookies. I just made them. It's a new recipe I wanted to try out before I start making the big batches." She handed the bag to Nikki, who opened the top and peered inside.

"What are they?"

"You're not allergic to nuts, are you?"

Nikki shook her head.

"Then I'm not going to say. When you've

had a few, let me know if you like them and your guess at the ingredients."

"Okay," Nikki drawled, arching her brows. Her eyes darted to the clock.

"Am I keeping you from something?" Sheila asked, noting the movement.

Shrugging apologetically, Nikki said, "I'm sorry. I just need to shower and change into something presentable before a video interview."

Sheila's shoulders straightened. "Like…a job interview?"

"Yes."

"A job you could commute to?"

"I'm sure I could do the planning from home, but I'd have to be onsite for the actual execution. Oh." Nikki breathed out the syllable, spotting the look on Sheila's face. "I was only supposed to be here through the New Year," Nikki reminded her. The reminder struck Nikki hard, almost made her wince.

"I know."

"And the job, if I take it, is in Vermont."

"I see," said Sheila. "Would this be a good move for you?"

"It might be," Nikki answered softly. "It might be the type of position I've dreamt about. I won't know for sure until I speak with Mary and a couple others who will be in on the meeting."

"If it makes you happy, Nikki, do it. We all deserve to be happy. But know you will be missed, my dear, by everyone you've met."

Nikki drew a deep breath, let it out. "Thank

you, Sheila. I'll miss you all, too." She meant it, more than she could have imagined. "I'll let you know as soon as I know."

"And about those cookies. I need to know that, too."

"Of course!" Laughing, she walked Sheila to the door and saw her out. As soon as she closed the door behind the woman, Nikki found herself wiping tears from her face.

*   *   *

The minute Nikki signed off from the online meeting/interview, she shoved in three cookies in a row, followed more slowly by the fourth, trying to analyze the taste and contents. Not being an accomplished baker herself, she didn't find it easy. Hazelnut. Chocolate. White chocolate chips. She could see those, at least. Some type of liqueur. Coffee, perhaps?

Considering she'd eaten four in short order, she felt confident telling Sheila her cookies were delicious, although less confident about ingredients. As for the job, she wasn't ready to talk about it at all.

It was perfect for her, no denying. But the fact she hesitated, and asked to let them know following the holidays—to which they readily agreed—gave her pause. Vermont was a beautiful area. Anywhere in Vermont. As she'd expected, she could work from home except those periods when her presence would be necessary to assure execution. The stores under their company would all require her services throughout the year due to change of season, change of product, sometimes change of management. A constant, artistic challenge. What could be better?

And, she reminded herself, she couldn't beat the money offered. She could never expect the same elsewhere, and certainly not as her own boss.

Peeking into the paper bag to see how many cookies remained, Nikki chided herself not to eat anymore. They were worth savoring, after all. Plus, she had clearly scarfed them down because she was upset. By what? Good news? Except, the news also included another move, a more permanent one. Despite her waffling, deep inside she'd decided she would like to stay in Connor Falls. The place felt like home in a way nothing had in a good many years.

How much of that had to do with Rory? Not all that much, really. She liked everyone she'd met, loved the area, enjoyed the town's vibe, its people. But if she let herself get closer to Rory in these next few weeks and things didn't work out, how awkward that would be. If she let herself get closer to him at all, how much more difficult would her decision to move states away become?

Growling like a hamster with a mouth full of nuts, and realizing in that instant another cookie had made its way into hers, Nikki texted Sheila with her guess as to the ingredients, told her the cookies were fabulous and went on to mention the interview had gone well but she hadn't made up her mind.

There, she thought, tossing the phone onto the counter. No commitment. Not yet.

Crumpling the paper down tightly around the remaining cookie, Nikki shoved the bag into the cabinet. Afterward, she emailed herself the Christmas list she'd made, so she could open it on her phone. She decided she may as well do some shopping right then, although before she left the cottage she also texted Reese and let him know she'd join the caroling in the park. She had to make the best memories while she still could.

That thought stopped her cold. It appeared very telling. Yet she would have to dismiss those reservations if she were going to properly consider the job offer. She doubted another like it would come along again. She had a lot to think about. A lot.

Getting into her car, she did what she normally would when a decision needed to be made. She went for a pointless, no-destination ride.

Everywhere she went, she drove past open farmland, woods, small communities, and little villages still charming after the many years since they obviously came to being. Not all that far away, she came to a much larger town than Connor Falls and drove slowly through it, first looking at the businesses and their window displays—she couldn't help it—and then down the side streets, eyeing the houses. Unfortunately, any contemplation focused on what she saw rather than what she needed to think about. Her go-to practice wasn't helping.

Finally leaving the bigger town behind, Nikki took a turn, intending to drive back to Connor Falls. She had no idea, however, where she'd ended up. Pulling off the narrow highway onto a small side road, Nikki set her in-car map, waited for it to catch up, and went on her way again, spying more sights and scenery and communities to enamor her. In time, she recognized her surroundings. A short second later, she experienced panic. She was about to drive by Rory's house.

She kept her eyes straight ahead. She could pretend, if he happened to be looking out his window, that she didn't know. At the last moment, however, she pivoted her head to check his driveway. Even without further assessment, something told her he wasn't home. Of course, she then began to wonder where he might be.

"Stop it," she said out loud, remembering an instant later he had mentioned another job. A short-term one. Finishing a basement the owner had started. Right.

Letting out a breath, she drove on into town. After she finished shopping, she would do her thinking at home.

At *home*.

The decision that really shouldn't be anything but an obvious choice wasn't going to be easy at all.

Chapter Twenty-Four

Rory hung up, frowning at his cell phone as he lowered it to the table. This was the third call he'd gotten about caroling in the park this afternoon. The third call, and none happened to be from Nikki. He hadn't spoken to her since last Saturday at the pub. The night he kissed her.

He shouldn't have done it. Not because of Kat, but because of all the talk about Kat and still fighting with grief, and not being ready. Maybe not all those things were discussed out loud, but they were implied. Wafted about in the air between him and everything else. Between him and Nikki. Except there was no him and Nikki. They had become friends, sure. The kiss had been inappropriate and badly timed.

It hadn't felt that way, though. Remembering it again, he definitely knew it hadn't felt that way.

Annoyed with himself, he stormed over to the kitchen sink and rinsed the dishes he'd piled in there from breakfast and lunch. A vigorous rinsing, followed by an aggressive stacking into the dishwasher. Followed by a blank stare out the kitchen window toward the fields across the street, a frying pan still clutched in his hand.

He could help out with the caroling this evening. Why not? No costumes involved. Not that he'd made much effort with his for the thing at Luke's. The old top hat was something he'd had around for ages. He might wear the hat anyway, for the heck of it. He might pin a flower to his coat, too, if he could find one. Nikki would get the reference. But he wasn't sure she'd be there. Even if she came, the flower would imply something between them that didn't exist. Or shouldn't.

Because he'd gotten that call, too. From Sheila. Telling him Nikki had received a great job offer she was contemplating. Sheila hadn't called only to tell him this. She didn't gossip, Sheila didn't. The news had come out in a roundabout way, when they were discussing something else. Something he couldn't remember anymore. The only thing he recalled from the conversation pertained to Nikki and the job waiting for her.

Releasing a held breath, Rory slowly lowered the pan into the sink and started scrubbing it, picturing the miles between Connor Falls and anywhere in Vermont.

*   *   *

Nikki had asked. And asked again, just to be sure. No costume needed. She could dress as warmly as she liked. A good thing, because even though Rory's personally forecasted snow hadn't arrived yet—except in sprinkles here and gone—the night promised to be quite cold. She hadn't heard from Rory, not even a text, but that was okay. She'd left him alone, too, to work on his life. For her, the job decision needed to be practical, not emotional. This wasn't just a job for her to do, but a placement in a company. Giving up her own business was a big decision, and the fact she hadn't already jumped in with both feet troubled her. She would need to list pros and cons. She'd always viewed those lists as tedious, but perhaps times existed when such tactics became crucial.

Locking her car, Nikki strode in the park's direction. The sun was nearly down. On every lamppost, lighted wreaths hung. More lights twinkled in windows. Many people on the sidewalks greeted her in passing. Those who didn't seemed preoccupied but not rude. It was the Christmas season, so not surprising. Nikki would have found the sidewalks surrounding her former home much the same. As for Vermont, she had no idea what the people there were like. She had to stop looking for comparisons and stick with the facts.

Voices warmed up in song inside the park. Nikki heard them as she approached. She quickened her pace. Once inside, she took her place among the gathered carolers, opening the sheet music packet thrust in her hands. For the first half hour or so, Nikki's voice mingled with the others. They all strolled together mainly to keep warm, smiling and singing for those who entered the park. After breaking for hot beverage provided by a nearby restaurant, they readied to start again.

"Mind if I share?"

Nikki jerked around. Rory stood at her back, pointing at the sheet music in her hand. "You're here," she said unnecessarily.

"I'm a bit late. I waited for a break before coming over. I didn't want to interrupt."

Nikki couldn't deny being happy to see him. She didn't even try. Her stomach twisted into a knot.

"Have you eaten?" he asked.

"Not yet."

"Maybe after—"

Interrupted by Reese announcing they had one minute before the next round, Rory and Nikki joined the others. Rory bent close to Nikki's ear.

"Dinner?" he said. "A late snack?"

Nikki nodded, fighting the flush brought on by his breath moving over her cheek. He seemed unaware as he straightened. Staying beside her due to their shared music, he matched his steps to hers as they moved through the park. When the singing concluded at seven o'clock, Nikki turned her sheets in and declined an invitation for another evening at the pub. Rory did the same.

"There's a diner outside of town," Nikki said. "Sleepy's, I think it's called."

"I know it," said Rory.

"Why don't we grab a bite there?" For some reason, Nikki didn't want to tell him about her possible future plans here in Connor Falls. But she planned to tell him. There was every reason to do so, and no reason not to.

They headed down the same street, side by side. He'd parked closer than she had, and paused outside his pickup. "We can ride together and I'll bring you back to your car after."

"It's out of your way. I'll meet you. It's fine."

If he noticed her awkward delivery, he made no mention. Nikki continued to her car, glancing back once. Rory continued to stand outside the pickup's door. Seeing her watching him, he raised his hand in a quick wave and got in.

Nikki realized in that instant Rory had already heard her news. Word-of-mouth, probably from Sheila to Pete to who-knew-who. A downfall from living in a small, closeknit community. Yet Connor Falls wasn't that small. And maybe not even that closeknit. But it was special. She'd recognized the quality the moment she arrived.

In her vehicle, Nikki grasped the wheel with both hands, biting her lip and staring out along the street. Rory passed in his truck with a light toot on the horn. She gave him a quick smile he couldn't possibly see and waited in her car until he had turned the corner. Yanking her phone from her purse, she sent a text to Mary before pulling away from the curb to follow Rory from town.

*　　*　　*

The diner wasn't that crowded, giving Rory the opportunity to wait outside for Nikki rather than get a table first. He saw her pull into a spot not far from his truck and walked over to her car.

"Hi," he said as she got out.

"Hi." An awkward silence followed and his heart plummeted into his stomach in a way he hadn't experienced in quite a while. "Crab cakes are their specialty," he said. "Do you like crab cakes?"

"I do. Let's see what else is on the menu, but I might have to give theirs a try."

He held the diner door for her, walked at her back, noticed her height and how the light shone on her hair. He noted her odd posture, too. She didn't seem quite so comfortable in his presence as he was used to. His mouth twisted.

They were shown to a booth in the back, somewhat private due to the momentary lack in patronage. Nikki picked up her menu first, holding it close to her face. Very quickly, she set it down. Rory waited with hands folded across his own.

"I received a job offer," said Nikki, "but you know that, don't you?"

"Sheila mentioned it," he answered in a deliberately offhand manner. "Is it a good one?"

"It's...something I never expected to come my way."

"So, you'll take it," Rory stated. Why shouldn't she? Her expression made it clear she wanted to.

"It's a big company. I'd be working for them rather than for myself. But I'd have guaranteed income, benefits, paid time off, all of that."

"Sounds perfect." As much as he believed those words, he had to force them out to be heard by her. Nikki gazed at him, lips compressed. She rocked her head a little from side to side. After a second or two, she straightened and spoke again.

"I had a quick conversation with Mary in the car on my way over here. If I can get a ticket, I'll fly out tomorrow to check everything out in person, have a more in-depth discussion, take a look around the area. Make up my mind. There's no reason to put it off. I really ought to know what I want, right?"

Odd question. Rory slid his menu in a small circle on the tabletop. "Will you be coming back to Connor Falls for Christmas?" he heard himself ask.

"Of course," she said. "I wouldn't miss it."

Rory huffed out a nearly silent breath. "Good. I'm happy for you, Nikki. Let me know how it goes."

He spoke the truth, yet his guts recoiled as if from a hefty, steel-fisted punch.

Chapter Twenty-Five

The night before departure, Nikki had done some reading about Vermont. Apparently, it was the second least populous state in the country. A mental check mark went on the pro side. In two-thousand sixteen, it ranked as the safest state. Another check mark had appeared in her head. Oh, and Burlington, the largest city, was a year prior to that safety ranking the first in the United States to operate on renewable energy completely. All pluses. She wasn't going to Burlington, though. Her destination happened to be Rutland, a somewhat smaller city located quite close to New York and Massachusetts, and one for which she could not get a timely, direct flight into their airport. She decided to drive. With optimal driving conditions, the trip hadn't taken much more than five hours. Nikki enjoyed driving. Always had. Plus, she needed, wanted, and was determined to get on with her decision-making.

Now, she stood before the huge window in her hotel room, staring out to the nearby mountains. The drive in had revealed scene after scene marked by picturesque beauty. The city itself, much larger than smalltown Connor Falls, was nevertheless charming. As she gazed toward the beautiful mountains, already white with snow for skiing, Nikki found herself thinking about practical matters, like expenses in the area. Even this could be considered a plus, as Rutland's cost of living was nearly ten percent lower than the average in both the country and the state. In a few minutes, she'd get a feel for the residents, too, when she set out on her fifteen-minute walk to meet Mary.

Right now, though, after having spent her recent time in Connor Falls, she felt like a stranger in a strange land. To be expected, she told herself. No place was like home the second you entered. Immediately upon having that thought, her mind went to the little rented cottage, to the people she'd met in Connor Falls. To Gina. Tessa. Sheila and Pete. Lyddie, Luke.

Rory.

Well, maybe some places could feel like home. Even so, she wouldn't base important decisions on her emotional reaction to Connor Falls and the people she'd come to know there, especially considering the upheaval of her life prior. Taking a deep breath, Nikki reached for her phone to shut off the quietly chirping reminder.

Time to go. She checked her hair, her teeth, and bundled into her coat and scarf, setting off to greet what might very well be her new life.

*   *   *

Two hours later, after a tour through the lovely old building containing the corporate offices, introductions to the friendly others who worked there, the scheduled meeting with Mary, Dan and Sylvan, including a slideshow revealing the various ski shops, clothing stores, and numerous other establishments they owned or provided services to, Nikki, her head jammed with more information than she could wrap her thoughts around, accompanied Mary to a nearby coffee shop for further discussion.

Now, clutching a cup filled with warm, fragrant brew, Nikki watched Mary through the window. Mary had excused herself to take a call, which she'd opted to engage in out on the sidewalk. Nikki sat alone, breathing in the coffee's scent, enjoying the cup's warmth in her chilled hand, and fighting an overwhelming sense of imposter syndrome.

Nikki had been advised by all three in the meeting that they wanted her for the position based on her initiative in her own business, her ongoing portfolio, her durable personality during the on-line meeting, and the credentials and accomplishments outlined in the *curriculum vitae* she kept permanently posted on LinkedIn and her website, without a real belief anyone would ever look at it. Mary had reached out earlier in the day to Tessa for her input as to Nikki's efforts in Hannah's windows and made sure Nikki heard a reiteration of Tessa's glowing report. What Nikki and Mary hoped to accomplish here in the coffee shop was hammering out the details to engage Nikki with the company.

Nikki had already been offered a salary amounting to two and half times what she'd made in her best year, been presented with the benefits package, engaged in discussion about what would be required from her. Nikki still had a question—well, several—to ask Mary once she came back inside. Nikki waited, cup pressed close to her face as she inhaled the captivating and oddly soothing fragrance. She had no idea what was in the coffee. Mary had ordered, stating Nikki would be surprised.

Nikki didn't particularly like surprises. This one seemed harmless enough, however. She sipped again, swallowed, watched Mary hang up and head back toward the door.

"Sorry about that," the woman apologized once inside.

"It's okay," Nikki answered. "Is everything all right?"

With a nod, Mary resumed her seat. "You had some more questions?"

"I do." Nikki set her cup down, positioning it so she could still smell the contents. "You mentioned several times that this is a vacant position. Would you mind telling me what happened to the person who held it before?"

Mary's lips curved in a small smile. "Not at all. Debbie retired. It was…time. Not because of age," Mary interjected when Nikki's brows lifted. "I think she lost interest. Burned out, maybe? She always kept up with what was on trend, but she'd stopped making trends of her own."

"That's a shame," Nikki responded. "When you love your work, you expect to always hold onto that feeling."

"Yes," Mary agreed. "And you still do. One can see that in all you've shared in your portfolio and the way you spoke about your work the other day and this afternoon, in person."

Nikki nodded, slowly. "Nothing's changed about me working from my home and coming in as necessary, right? Because I have to be honest. I'm not an office kind of girl."

"Whatever you need."

Nikki's gaze shifted to the window. To a man passing by. Something in the way he moved made her remember Rory crossing the driveway on his way to his in-laws. She shifted her thoughts away from the recollection and back to Mary. The woman was reaching into the portfolio she'd carried with her from the meeting.

"I have the offer letter here," she said, withdrawing several pages from inside and placing them on the table. "You can read it through and sign it, and we'll get this whole thing going."

Nikki spun the papers around, placed her hands flat on them. "Just a couple more questions," she said.

Mary laughed. "Of course. Like I said, whatever you need. We don't want to lose you."

Chapter Twenty-Six

Rory followed Sheila down the pathway from her front door as he headed for his truck. Sheila jingled the key to the cottage in her hand. He could tell she was more upset than she let on. So was he.

"I'll miss her," Sheila muttered before turning down the pathway to the cottage door.

"Me, too," said Rory, and caught himself. Sheila paused, looking at him. He cleared his throat. "I hope it's okay to say that to you."

Sheila's mouth turned up, her eyes glittering with unshed tears. She lifted her arms. He stepped into her embrace, wrapped his own arms around her in the heavy plaid jacket she favored.

"Goodness, Rory," she whispered, "of course it is. There's no one on this earth or above it who would wish for you to remain lonely the rest of your life."

Rory wouldn't let her pull away until he'd dashed a hand across his eyes several times. When he released her, he bent and planted a kiss on her chilled cheek. "I love you, you know."

Her smiling lips quivered. "I love you, too." She shoved him lightly away. "Now, get on with yourself. I've got things to tend to."

Rory continued to his truck, opened the door and slipped behind the wheel, watching Sheila open the cottage door and disappear inside. So much could change in a person's life inside the smallest increment of time. Not a year, a week, a day. In a moment.

He recalled the night he'd looked up from gathering his things one last time in the cottage and saw Nikki Sharp walking in with Sheila. Nikki hadn't recognized him, but he'd known her right away. He'd understood as soon as his gaze landed on her that things weren't going to be the same.

Yes, he'd known in a moment. Only a moment. And now it was too late.

Pulling out onto the road, he headed straight for his brother's house, wanting to talk to him. Luke, infinitely more level-headed. Lights were on in the barn. The door stood slightly ajar. Rory parked and got out, stopping just outside. He didn't mean to eavesdrop. Lydia's voice and her words had caught his attention.

"Uncle Rory will come, don't you think? We haven't had a party in ever so long."

"I hope so," he heard Luke answer. "You might have to be the one to ask him, though. He won't be able to tell you no."

Lyddie giggled. "I'll explain it's a special party."

Rory yanked the door open. "What kind of special party?"

With a squeal, Lydia rushed him. He hoisted his niece into the air and settled her on his hip.

"A Christmas party," Lydia said.

"With costumes?" Rory teased her.

"No, silly." She paused a second, thinking. "Well, maybe. What do you think, Dad?"

"It's tomorrow night," Luke said, handing Rory a homemade apple cider from the refrigerator. "I don't think that's enough time."

"Tomorrow night?" Rory echoed. "Left the invite a bit late, didn't you?"

"We just decided this morning to do it."

Rory frowned. "And there are people actually coming?"

Luke poked his daughter in the belly. "Oh, yeah," he said. "Big pizza night. You'll have to get a gift. Nothing more than five dollars. We're going to do an exchange. It's not a big deal. And I think people went for it because it was last-minute and not the weekend, when everybody is all booked. No pressure."

"Wow," Rory said, eyeing his brother up and down. "Okay. I'll be there."

Lydia hugged him tight around the neck, pressing her cheek against his. "I knew you would!"

Rory set her down, took a swig from the bottle in his hand. Non-alcoholic cider. Leave it to Luke to make it, bottle it, keep such a thing around. It was cold and tasted good. He swallowed, remembering the scene outside Sheila and Pete's. Blinking, Rory turned to study something, anything, on the wall.

"You okay?" Luke asked.

Rory nodded a few times, slowly, not looking at him.

"I'm not so sure I believe you, but all right. Where's Nikki?"

Where's Nikki. As if they were a couple and she should be there with him. He let out a breath. Lyddie watched from her favorite perch on the table. Rory spotted her orange cat, Frank, plainly asleep nearby.

"She's in Vermont," Rory said.

"Vermont?" Lydia and Luke echoed simultaneously.

"Job."

"But—"

"She has a life," Rory said. "She's getting on with it. Some of us forgot how to do that. For too long, maybe."

"Lyddie," said Luke, "why don't you take Frank and head inside. I'll be along in a minute. It's almost dinnertime anyway."

"Uncle Rory, do you want to stay for dinner? It's leftovers. But they're good."

"Maybe," Rory answered. "If I don't, I'll see you tomorrow."

"Okay." She snatched the sleeping Frank into her arms and ran out the door.

Luke stepped nearer to him, touched his sleeve. "It'll be all right," he said.

Rory nodded again. "I know." His admission felt oddly like the truth.

*　　*　　*

The next evening, Rory dressed with a little more care than he'd given to clothing since Thanksgiving. Before that, well, he didn't want to think about it. Big pizza night or not, he might as well be seen to make the effort. He'd gone into town after work and bought a candle at Sophie's Chandlery. The store was having a sale on the small ones with bumped up glass tops, whatever they were called. Close enough to five dollars not to make a difference, and it was already in a little gift bag, so he didn't have to try to wrap the oddly shaped thing. Everyone loved a candle. Even when not being burned, they smelled nice left open, and this one had smelled great when he sniffed it at the store. Reminded him of cookies.

Rory glanced across the kitchen, spotting another candle with some surprise before he remembered it had been there for a long while. The last candle Kat had bought. Crossing the floor, he lifted the lid and bent to smell the fragrance. Cranberry. Her favorite. The wick had never been lit. There was some saying he couldn't bring to mind about candles not being lit. He reached for the stick matches in the closet, figuring he could at least give the wick a flame for a second, but he dropped his hand back to his side, wondering why he'd held onto the candle for all this time. Not in memory. That hadn't been the reason. He'd just stopped seeing it. Like so many things.

Smiling, he decided he would give the cranberry candle to Sheila and Pete. They could light it for their daughter Christmas Day. He'd promised to stop by for their Christmas brunch, and he had no plans to dodge the occasion. As for the actual gift for them both, Rory still hadn't figured it out. He needed to get a move on. Tonight, however, he was going to a party and, surprisingly, looking forward to it.

When he turned into Luke's lot, Rory glanced toward the house. No parking left up there. He pulled in by the barn beside a couple other vehicles instead, and hiked up the gravel driveway, the gift bag tucked under his arm. The porch was alight with multi-colored bulbs. A wreath hung on the door, and another on the large, front window. Rory's lips turned up. Two cut-out Santa faces were taped to the glass at either side, no doubt a contribution by Lydia. For a full minute, Rory stood in the colorful glow without going in, listening to the voices inside. The door opened abruptly and Lyddie's little hand reached out to his.

"Get in here, Uncle Rory. Hurry up."

Rory let her drag him forward. She released his hand and stepped around to shut the door behind him. Once she had, she grabbed his hand again, tugging him deeper into the room, much to everyone's amusement. He followed her lead dutifully, a crooked smile on his face, greeting people he knew as he passed them.

"Put the gift there," Lyddie said, pointing at a pile beneath the tree. When he didn't move fast enough, she took the bag from him and set it neatly down before grabbing his hand again. "And now, follow me some more."

"As if I had a choice," he mumbled at her. She

giggled.

He could see the back of Luke's dark head in the kitchen. Several people had gathered in the room. His brother appeared to be speaking to one in earnest. The woman stepped away, swept a knit cap from her head, turned in Rory's direction. Her mouth widened into a brilliant smile.

"There you go, Uncle Rory. She's here. I texted her," Lydia announced with pride.

Rory closed the gap between himself and Nikki in one step and pulled her close, bent his head, lowered his mouth over hers. Same as last time, but longer and so much better. People started to laughingly clear their throats.

"Sorry," Rory apologized, straightening. "We'll be right back. Nikki? Can we talk outside for a minute?"

"Talk. Right," someone called after them.

Nikki followed, her hand in his. Once outside, he kissed her again quite slowly. He found he could scarcely breathe. With an abrupt intake of air, he stopped kissing her and stepped back.

"You're here," he said.

Nikki laughed. "Not because of Lydia's text. I was already on my way. I told you I'd be back. Lydia's invite took me by surprise, though."

"I didn't hear much from you after you left. I got those pictures of the mountains. Not that I expected you to keep in touch. I figured you had a lot going on. Sheila's been keeping up with watering your Christmas tree," he finished his ramble, feeling foolish.

Nikki's eyes shone. She met his gaze. "Are you

going to ask?"

He blew out a breath, knowing exactly what she meant. "Okay. Yes. Did you get the job?"

She nodded.

His guts coiled like a snake getting ready to bite him where it hurt most. "Congratulations," he said, managing to sound like he meant it. Which he did. Of course, he did. But it still wasn't quite good news for him.

"I need to speak with Sheila and Pete," Nikki went on. "They weren't in when I got home."

Home. He only wished it was, for her. She had a life though. Had one before Connor Falls and would soon start another. "They'll miss you, too," he said, without thinking.

Nikki cocked her head to one side. Looking adorable and well-kissed, he had to admit. "Too?" she echoed.

He kept silent.

She sighed. "I need to speak with them about extending my stay, Rory, not shortening it. I'll eventually need a slightly bigger place, but right now, if they'll have me, I love the cottage."

"I—what?"

"I took the job, yes, but with certain provisions. Since they'd already agreed to my working from home, I saw no reason to change my location and I made sure they agreed to that in writing. I'll have to commute as necessary, but my physical presence is only required at certain times. So yes, I have the job, but I'm not going anywhere. Like I said, I love the cottage. I love Connor Falls. I've made good friends. And I'm quite fond of you, Rory. I think I could tell by that kiss you maybe feel the same?"

Nikki's gaze slid past his as she asked the question, moving to the window. She burst out laughing. Rory turned his head, finding more than Santa faces plastered to the glass. Everyone quickly cleared away. Rory spun back to her.

"I do," he said, and kissed her again for good measure.

*   *   *

Nikki bent and watered her tree, pressing her nose close to the needles to breathe in their scent. Afterward, she straightened, stretched, pivoted full circle, taking in the cottage around her. Sheila and Pete had agreed to the extension, month to month, but encouraged her to stay as long as she liked. Sheila had hugged her at the conversation's conclusion, holding on a bit too long. Both she and Nikki had pulled away teary-eyed.

Nikki had filed to change her address on-line to the PO Box she opened in Connor Falls. Knowing Connor Falls would now be her permanent address provided her with a bigger sense she belonged. As if she needed anything else to make her feel she'd found her home.

Home. And Christmas. What could be better?

Somebody suddenly knocked on the door. Not Sheila's musical knock. Something staccato, brisk, yet soft.

Rory.

Nikki hurried to the door and opened it. The wind blew in and Rory followed, his dark-brown hair damp, his coat shoulders, too. Bits of ice glittered in the folds and, she noticed when she looked down, his boots.

"You're not dressed," he said.

"Sure I am. I'm dressed for comfort, cozying up by the fire comfort. A cross between pjs and, I don't know, chopping wood. I am technically on vacation until the new year." She smirked at him. "Wait. You're all wet."

His brows arched. "It's snowing outside. Haven't you noticed?"

"It is?" Nikki ran to the window, peered out. She should have known. She should have recognized the softer edge to sound, the light hiss of flakes on glass. She should have looked outside at least once that morning, for goodness' sake. "It is!" she cried.

"My camera is in the truck. Where's yours? Or you could use your phone this time. I see it's on the charger. We're good to go. Photo ops, Nikki. Like I promised."

Nikki's grin stretched until she thought it might snap. She raced up the stairs to get fully outfitted. When she returned downstairs, Rory had worked apart the small fire so the logs lay lightly smoking apart from each other and the embers were banked. He shut the glass doors on them.

"I'll ask Sheila to check on this in a bit, but it should be fine," said Rory. "Ready?"

Nikki stomped into her boots, pulled her hat over her hair, snatched her gloves and phone from the counter. "Ready. More than ready."

"Me, too," he said. "Finally."

Nikki fit her fingers into his. Hand in hand, they walked out to greet the snowy, exciting, promising, heartwarming world they both called home.

Titles in the Connor Falls Christmas Series:

Hurry Home for Christmas
Connor Falls Christmas Book One

I Knew in a Moment
Connor Falls Christmas Book Two

Winter Light
A Connor Falls Christmas Novella

Light the Heart Home
A Connor Falls Christmas Novella

Home for the Holidays
A Connor Falls Christmas Novella

When the Heart Brings You Home
A Connor Falls Christmas Collection
containing *Winter Light, Light the
Heart Home,* and *Home for the
Holidays* in one volume

www.ingramcontent.com/pod-product-compliance
Lightning Source LLC
Chambersburg PA
CBHW032020310726
48972CB00002B/485